Thomas Hood

The Poetical Works

Vol. III

SALZWASSER VERLAG

Thomas Hood

The Poetical Works

Vol. III

Reprint of the original, first published in 1863.

1st Edition 2022 | ISBN: 978-3-37500-263-3

Verlag (Publisher): Salzwasser Verlag GmbH, Zeilweg 44, 60439 Frankfurt, Deutschland
Vertretungsberechtigt (Authorized to represent): E. Roepke, Zeilweg 44, 60439 Frankfurt, Deutschland
Druck (Print): Books on Demand GmbH, In de Tarpen 42, 22848 Norderstedt, Deutschland

THE POETICAL WORKS OF THOMAS HOOD.

WITH SOME ACCOUNT OF THE AUTHOR.

IN FOUR VOLUMES.

VOLUME III.

BOSTON

M.DCCC.LXIII.

CONTENTS.

VOL. III.

POEMS.

THE LOST HEIR.

" Oh where, and oh where
Is my bonny laddie gone ? "—OLD SONG.

ONE day, as I was going by
That part of Holborn christened High,
I heard a loud and sudden cry
That chilled my very blood;
And lo! from out a dirty alley,
Where pigs and Irish wont to rally,
I saw a crazy woman sally,
Bedaubed with grease and mud.
She turned her East, she turned her West,
Staring like Pythoness possest,
With streaming hair and heaving breast
As one stark mad with grief.
This way and that she wildly ran,
Jostling with woman and with man—
Her right hand held a frying pan,
The left a lump of beef.
At last her frenzy seemed to reach
A point just capable of speech,
And with a tone almost a screech,
As wild as ocean birds,
Or female Ranter moved to preach,
She gave her "sorrow words."

"O Lord! O dear, my heart will break, I shall
go stick stark staring wild!
Has ever a one seen any thing about the streets
like a crying lost-looking child?
Lawk help me, I don't know where to look, or to
run, if I only knew which way—
A Child as is lost about London streets, and especially
Seven Dials, is a needle in a bottle
of hay.
I am all in a quiver—get out of my sight, do,
you wretch, you little Kitty M'Nab!
You promised to have half an eye to him, you
know you did, you dirty deceitful young drab.
The last time as ever I see him, poor thing, was
with my own blessed Motherly eyes,
Sitting as good as gold in the gutter, a playing at
making little dirt pies.
I wonder he left the court where he was better
off than all the other young boys,
With two bricks, an old shoe, nine oyster-shells,
and a dead kitten by way of toys.
When his Father comes home, and he always
comes home as sure as ever the clock strikes
one,
He'll be rampant, he will, at his child being lost;
and the beef and the inguns not done!
La bless you, good folks, mind your own consarns,
and don't be making a mob in the street;
O serjeant M'Farlane! you have not come across
my poor little boy, have you, in your beat?

Do, good people, move on! don't stand staring at
me like a parcel of stupid stuck pigs;
Saints forbid! but he's p'r'aps been inviggled
away up a court for the sake of his clothes
by the prigs;
He'd a very good jacket, for certain, for I bought
it myself for a shilling one day in Rag Fair;
And his trowsers considering not very much
patched, and red plush, they was once his
Father's best pair.
His shirt, it's very lucky I'd got washing in the
tub, or that might have gone with the rest;
But he'd got on a very good pinafore with only
two slits and a burn on the breast.
He'd a goodish sort of hat, if the crown was
sewed in, and not quite so much jagg'd at the
brim.
With one shoe on, and the other shoe is a boot,
and not a fit, and you'll know by that if it's
him.
Except being so well dressed, my mind would mis-
give, some old beggar woman in want of an
orphan,
Had borrowed the child to go a begging with, but
I'd rather see him laid out in his coffin!
Do, good people, move on, such a rabble of boys!
I'll break every bone of 'em I come near,
Go home — you're spilling the porter — go
home — Tommy Jones, go along home with
your beer.

This day is the sorrowfullest day of my life, ever since my name was Betty Morgan,
Them vile Savoyards! they lost him once before all along of following a Monkey and an Organ:
O my Billy — my head will turn right round — if he 's got kiddynapped with them Italians,
They 'll make him a plaster parish image boy, they will, the outlandish tatterdemalions.
Billy — where are you, Billy? — I 'm as hoarse as a crow, with screaming for ye, you young sorrow!
And shan't have half a voice, no more I shan't, for crying fresh herrings to-morrow.
O Billy, your 're bursting my heart in two, and my life won't be of no more vally,
If I 'm to see other folk's darlins, and none of mine, playing like angels in our alley,
And what shall I do but cry out my eyes, when I looks at the old three-legged chair
As Billy used to make coach and horses of, and there a'n't no Billy there!
I would run all the wide world over to find him, if I only know'd where to run;
Little Murphy, now I remember, was once lost for a month through stealing a penny bun, —
The Lord forbid of any child of mine! I think it would kill me raily,
To find my Bill holdin' up his little innocent hand at the Old Bailey.

For though I say it as oughtn't, yet I will say, you may search for miles and mileses
And not find one better brought up, and more pretty behaved, from one end to t' other of St. Giles's.
And if I called him a beauty, it 's no lie, but only as a Mother ought to speak;
You never set eyes on a more handsomer face, only it hasn't been washed for a week;
As for hair, tho' its red, its the most nicest hair when I 've time to just show it the comb;
I 'll owe 'em five pounds, and a blessing besides, as will only bring him safe and sound home.
He 's blue eyes, and not to be called a squint, though a little cast he 's certainly got;
And his nose is still a good un, tho' the bridge is broke, by his falling on a pewter pint pot;
He 's got the most elegant wide mouth in the world, and very large teeth for his age;
And quite as fit as Mrs. Murdockson's child to play Cupid on the Drury Lane Stage.
And then he has got such dear winning ways — but O I never never shall see him no more!
O dear! to think of losing him just after nussing him back from death's door!
Only the very last month when the windfalls, hang 'em, was at twenty a penny!
And the threepence he 'd got by grottoing was spent in plums, and sixty for a child is too many.

And the Cholera man came and whitewashed us all and, drat him, made a seize of our hog.—
It 's no use to send the Cryer to cry him about, he 's such a blunderin' drunken old dog;
The last time he was fetched to find a lost child, he was guzzling with his bell at the Crown,
And went and cried a boy instead of a girl, for a distracted Mother and Father about Town.
Billy — where are you, Billy, I say? come Billy, come home, to your best of Mothers!
I 'm scared when I think of them Cabroleys, they drive so, they 'd run over their own Sisters and Brothers.
Or may be he 's stole by some chimbly sweeping wretch, to stick fast in narrow flues and what not,
And be poked up behind with a picked pointed pole, when the soot has ketched, and the chimbly 's red hot.
Oh I 'd give the whole wide world, if the world was mine, to clap my two longin' eyes on his face.
For he 's my darlin of darlins, and if he don't soon come back, you 'll see me drop stone dead on the place.
I only wish I 'd got him safe in these two Motherly arms, and wouldn't I hug him and kiss him!
Lawk! I never knew what a precious he was — but a child don't not feel like a child till you miss him.

Why there he is! Punch and Judy hunting, the young wretch, it's that Billy as sartin as sin!
But let me get him home, with a good grip of his hair, and I'm blest if he shall have a whole bone in his skin!

AN ANCIENT CONCERT.

BY A VENERABLE DIRECTOR.

" Give me *old* music — let me hear
The songs of *days* gone by!" — H. F. CHORLEY.

O! COME, all ye who love to hear
An ancient song in ancient taste,
To whom all bygone Music 's dear
As verdant spots in Memory's waste!
Its name "The Ancient Concert" wrongs,
And has not hit the proper clef,
To wit, Old Folks, to sing Old Songs,
To Old Subscribers rather deaf.

Away, then, Hawes! with all your band.
Ye beardless boys, this room desert!
One youthful voice, or youthful hand,
Our concert-pitch would disconcert!

No Bird must join our "vocal throng,"
The present age beheld at font:
Away, then, all ye "Sons of Song,"
Your Fathers are the men we want!

Away, Miss Birch, you 're in your prime!
Miss Romer, seek some other door!
Go, Mrs. Shaw! till, counting time,
You count you 're nearly fifty-four!
Go, Miss Novello, sadly young!
Go, thou composing Chevalier,
And roam the county towns among,
No Newcome will be welcome here!

Our Concert aims to give at *night*
The music that has had its *day!*
So, Rooke, for us you cannot write
Till time has made you Raven gray.
Your score may charm a modern ear,
Nay, ours, when three or fourscore old,
But in this Ancient atmosphere,
Fresh airs like yours would give us cold!

Go, Hawes, and Cawse, and Woodyat, go!
Hence, Shirreff, with those native curls
And Master Coward ought to know
This is no place for boys and girls!
No Massons here we wish to see;
Nor is it Mrs. Seguin's sphere,

And Mrs. B——! Oh! Mrs. B——,
Such Bishops are not reverend here!

What! Grisi, bright and beaming thus!
To sing the songs gone gray with age!
No, Grisi, no,—but come to us
And welcome, when you leave the stage!
Off, Ivanhoff!—till weak and harsh!—
Rubini, hence! with all the clan!
But come, Lablache, years hence, Lablache
A little shrivelled thin old man.

Go, Mr. Phillips, where you please!
Away, Tom Cooke, and all your batch;
You'd run us out of breath with Glees,
And Catches that we could not catch.
Away, ye Leaders all, who lead
With violins, quite modern things;
To guide our Ancient band we need
Old fiddles out of leading strings!

But come, ye Songsters, overripe,
That into "childish trebles break!"
And bring, Miss Winter, bring the pipe
That cannot sing without a shake!
Nay, come, ye Spinsters all, that spin
A slender thread of ancient voice,
Old notes that almost seem called in;
At such as you we *shall* rejoice!

No thund'ring Thalbergs here shall baulk,
Or ride your pet *D-cadence* o'er,
But fingers with a little chalk
Shall, moderato, keep the score!
No Broadwoods here so full of tone,
But Harpsichords assist the strain:
No Lincoln's pipes, we have our own
Bird-Organ, built by Tubal-Cain.

And welcome! St. Cecilians, now
Ye willy-nilly, ex-good fellows,
Who will strike up, no matter how,
With organs that survive their bellows!
And bring, O bring, your ancient styles
In which our elders loved to roam,
Those flourishes that strayed for miles,
Till some good fiddle led them home!

O come, ye ancient London Cries,
When Christmas Carols erst were sung!
Come, Nurse, who droned the lullabies,
"When Music, heavenly Maid, was young!"
No matter how the critics treat,
What modern sins and faults detect,
The Copy-Book shall still repeat,
These Concerts must "Command respect!"

A REPORT FROM BELOW.

"Blow high, blow low." — SEA SONG.

As Mister B. and Mistress B.
One night were sitting down to tea,
With toast and muffins hot —
They heard a loud and sudden bounce,
That made the very china flounce,
They could not for a time pronounce
If they were safe or shot —
For Memory brought a deed to match
At Deptford done by night —
Before one eye appeared a Patch
In t'other eye a Blight!

To be belaboured out of life,
Without some small attempt at strife,
Our nature will not grovel;
One impulse moved both man and dame,
He seized the tongs — she did the same,
Leaving the ruffian, if he came,
The poker and the shovel.

Suppose the couple standing so,
When rushing footsteps from below
Made pulses fast and fervent,

And first burst in the frantic cat,
All steaming like a brewer's rat,
And then — as white as my cravat —
Poor Mary May, the servant!

Lord, how the couple's teeth did chatter,
Master and Mistress both flew at her,
"Speak! Fire? or Murder? What's the matter?"
Till Mary getting breath,
Upon her tale began to touch
With rapid tongue, full trotting, such
As if she thought she had too much
To tell before her death: —
"We was both, Ma'am, in the wash-house, Ma'am, a-standing at our tubs,
And Mrs. Round was seconding what little things I rubs;
'Mary,' says she to me, 'I say' — and there she stops for coughin',
'That dratted copper flue has took to smokin' very often,
But please the pigs,' — for that's her way of swearing in a passion,
'I'll blow it up, and not be set a coughin' in this fashion!'
Well, down she takes my master's horn — I mean his horn for loading,
And empties every grain alive for to set the flue exploding.

Lawk, Mrs. Round! says I, and stares, that
quantum is unproper.
I 'm sartin sure it can't not take a pound to sky
a copper;
You 'll powder both our heads off, so I tells you,
with its puff,
But she only dried her fingers, and she takes a
pinch of snuff.
Well, when the pinch is over—'Teach your
grandmother to suck
A powder-horn,' says she—Well, says I, I wish
you luck.
Them words sets up her back, so with her hands
upon her hips,
'Come,' says she, quite in a huff, 'come, keep your
tongue inside your lips;
Afore ever you was born, I was well used to
things like these;
I shall put it in the grate, and let it burn up by
degrees.
So in it goes, and Bounce—O Lord! it gives us
such a rattle,
I thought we both were canonized, like Sogers in
a battle!
Up goes the copper like a squib, and us on both
our backs,
And bless the tubs, they bundled off, and split all
into cracks.
Well, there I fainted dead away, and might have
been cut shorter,

But Providence was kind, and brought me to with scalding water.
I first looks round for Mrs. Round, and sees her at a distance,
As stiff as starch, and looked as dead as any thing in existence;
All scorched and grimed, and more than that, I sees the copper slap
Right on her head, for all the world like a percussion copper cap.
Well, I crooks her little fingers, and crumps them well up together,
As humanity pints out, and burnt her nostrums with a feather:
But for all as I can do, to restore her to her mortality,
She never gives a sign of a return to sensuality.
Thinks I, well there she lies, as dead as my own late departed mother,
Well, she 'll wash no more in this world, whatever she does in t'other.
So I gives myself to scramble up the linens for a minute,
Lawk, sich a shirt! thinks I, it's well my master wasn't in it;
Oh! I never, never, never, never, never, see a sight so shockin';
Here lays a leg, and there a leg — I mean, you know, a stocking —
Bodies all slit and torn to rags, and many a tattered skirt,

And arms burnt off, and sides and backs all
scotched and black with dirt;
But as nobody was in 'em — none but — nobody
was hurt!
Well, there I am, a-scrambling up the things, all
in a lump,
When, mercy on us! such a groan as makes my
heart to jump.
And there she is, a-lying with a crazy sort of
eye,
A-staring at the wash-house roof, laid open to the
sky:
Then she beckons with a finger, and so down to
her I reaches,
And puts my ear agin her mouth to hear her
dying speeches,
For, poor soul! she has a husband and young
orphans, as I knew;
Well, Ma'am, you won't believe it, but it's Gos-
pel fact and true,
But these words is all she whispered — 'Why,
where *is* the powder blew?'"

ODE TO M. BRUNEL.*

"Well said old Mole! canst work i' the dark so fast? a worthy pioneer! — HAMLET.

WELL !——Monsieur Brunel,
How prospers now thy mighty undertaking,
To join by a hollow way the Bankside friends
Of Rotherhithe, and Wapping, —
Never be stopping,
But poking, groping, in the dark keep making
An archway, underneath the Dabs and Gudgeons,
For Collier men and pitchy old Curmudgeons,
To cross the water in inverse proportion,
Walk under steamboats under the keel's ridge,
To keep down all extortion,
And without sculls to diddle London Bridge !
In a fresh hunt, a new Great Bore to worry,
Thou didst to earth thy human terriers follow,
Hopeful at last from Middlesex to Surrey,
To give us the "View hollow."
In short it was thy aim, right north and south,
To put a pipe into old Thames's mouth ;
Alas ! half-way thou hadst proceeded, when
Old Thames, through roof, not water-proof,
Came, like "a tide in the affairs of men ;"

* [M. Brunel was the architect of the Tunnel under the Thames, at London.]

And with a mighty stormy kind of roar,
Reproachful of thy wrong,
Burst out in that old song
Of Incledon's, beginning "Cease, rude Bore." —
Sad is it, worthy of one's tears,
Just when one seems the most successful,
To find one's self o'er head and ears
In difficulties most distressful!
Other great speculations have been nursed,
Till want of proceeds laid them on a shelf;
But thy concern was at the worst,
When it began to *liquidate* itself!
But now Dame Fortune has her false face hidden,
And languishes thy Tunnel, — so to paint,
Under a slow incurable complaint,
Bed-ridden!
Why, when thus Thames — bed-bothered — why repine!
Do try a spare bed at the Serpentine!
Yet let none think thee dazed, or crazed, or stupid;
And sunk beneath thy own and Thames's craft;
Let them not style thee some Mechanic Cupid
Pining and pouting o'er a broken shaft!
I 'll tell thee with thy tunnel what to do;
Light up thy boxes, build a bin or two,
The wine does better than such water trades:
Stick up a sign — the sign of the Bore's Head;
I 've drawn it ready for thee in black lead,
And make thy cellar subterrane, — Thy Shades!

OVER THE WAY.

"I sat over against a window where there stood a pot with very pretty flowers; and I had my eyes fixed on it, when on a sudden the window opened, and a young lady appeared whose beauty struck me." — ARABIAN NIGHTS.

ALAS! the flames of an unhappy lover
About my heart and on my vitals prey;
I've caught a fever that I can't get over,
Over the way!

Oh! why are eyes of hazel? noses Grecian?
I've lost my rest by night, my peace by day,
For want of some brown Holland or Venetian,
Over the way.

I've gazed too often, till my heart's as lost
As any needle in a stack of hay:
Crosses belong to love, and mine is crossed
Over the way!

I cannot read or write, or thoughts relax —
Of what avail Lord Althorp or Earl Grey?
They cannot ease me of *my* window-tax
Over the way!

Even on Sunday my devotions vary,
And from St. Bennet Fink they go astray
To dear St. Mary Overy — the Mary
Over the way!

Oh! if my godmother were but a fairy,
With magic wand, how I would beg and pray
That she would change me into that canary
Over the way!

I envy every thing that 's near Miss Lindo,
A pug, a poll, a squirrel or a jay —
Blest blue-bottles! that buzz about the window
Over the way!

Even at even, for there be no shutters,
I see her reading on, from grave to gay,
Some tale or poem, till the candle gutters
Over the way!

And then — oh! then — while the clear waxen taper
Emits, two stories high, a starlike ray,
I see twelve auburn curls put into paper
Over the way!

But how breathe unto her my deep regards,
Or ask her for a whispered ay or nay, —
Or offer her my hand, some thirty yards
Over the way?

Cold as the pole she is to my adoring; —
Like Captain Lyon, at Repulse's Bay,
I meet an icy end to my exploring
Over the way!

Each dirty little Savoyard that dances
She looks on — Punch — or chimney-sweeps in May;
Zounds! wherefore cannot I attract her glances
Over the way?

Half out she leans to watch a tumbling brat,
Or yelping cur, run over by a dray;
But I'm in love — she never pities that!
Over the way!

I go to the same church — a love-lost labour;
Haunt all her walks, and dodge her at the play;
She does not seem to know she has a neighbour
Over the way!

At private theatres she never acts;
No Crown-and-Anchor balls her fancy sway;
She never visits gentlemen with tracts
Over the way!

To billets-doux by post she shows no favour —
In short, there is no plot that I can lay
To break my window-pains to my enslaver
Over the way!

I play the flute, she heeds not my chromatics,
No friend an introduction can purvey;
I wish a fire would break out in the attics
Over the way!

My wasted form ought of itself to touch her;
My baker feels my appetite's decay;
And as for butcher's meat — oh! she's my butcher
Over the way!

At beef I turn; at lamb or veal I pout;
I never ring now to bring up the tray;
My stomach grumbles at my dining out
Over the way!

I'm weary of my life; without regret
I could resign this miserable clay
To lie within that box of mignonette
Over the way!

I've fitted bullets to my pistol-bore;
I've vowed at times to rush where trumpets bray,
Quite sick of number one — and number four
Over the way!

Sometimes my fancy builds up castles airy.
Sometimes it only paints a ferme orneé,
A horse, a cow, six fowls, a pig, and Mary,
Over the way!

Sometimes I dream of her in bridal white,
Standing before the altar, like a fay;
Sometimes of balls, and neighbourly invite
Over the way!

I've cooed with her in dreams, like any turtle,
I've snatched her from the Clyde, the Tweed, and
Tay;
Thrice I have made a grove of that one myrtle
Over the way!

Thrice I have rowed her in a fairy shallop,
Thrice raced to Gretna in a neat "po-shay,"
And showered crowns to make the horses gallop
Over the way!

And thrice I've started up from dreams appalling
Of killing rivals in a bloody fray —
There is a young man very fond of calling
Over the way!

Oh! happy man — above all kings in glory,
Whoever in her ear may say his say,
And add a tale of love to that one story
Over the way!

Nabob of Arcot — Despot of Japan —
Sultan of Persia — Emperor of Cathay —
Much rather would I be the happy man
Over the way!

With such a lot my heart would be in clover —
But what — O horror! — what do I survey!
Postilions and white favours! — all is over
Over the way!

A NOCTURNAL SKETCH.

A NEW STYLE OF BLANK VERSE.

Even is come; and from the dark Park, hark,
The signal of the setting sun — one gun!
And six is sounding from the chime, prime time
To go and see the Drury-Lane Dane slain, —
Or hear Othello's jealous doubt spout out, —
Or Macbeth raving at that shade-made blade,
Denying to his frantic clutch much touch; —
Or else to see Ducrow with wide stride ride
Four horses as no other man can span;
Or in the small Olympic Pit, sit split
Laughing at Liston, while you quiz his phiz.

Anon Night comes, and with her wings brings things
Such as, with his poetic tongue, Young sung;
The gas up-blazes with its bright white light,
And paralytic watchmen prowl, howl, growl,
About the streets and take up Pall-Mall Sal,

Who, hasting to her nightly jobs, robs fobs.
Now thieves to enter for your cash, smash, crash,
Past drowsy Charley, in a deep sleep, creep,
But frightened by Policeman B. 3, flee,
And while they 're going, whisper low, "No go!"

Now puss, while folks are in their beds, treads leads,
And sleepers waking, grumble — "Drat that cat!"
Who in the gutter caterwauls, squalls, mauls
Some feline foe, and screams in shrill ill-will.

Now Bulls of Bashan, of a prize size, rise
In childish dreams, and with a roar gore poor
Georgy, or Charley, or Billy, willy-nilly; —
But Nursemaid in a nightmare rest, chest-pressed,
Dreameth of one of her old flames, James Games,
And that she hears — what faith is man's — Ann's banns
And his, from Reverend Mr. Rice, twice, thrice:
White ribbons flourish, and a stout shout out,
That upward goes, shows Rose knows those bows' woes!

DOMESTIC ASIDES; OR, TRUTH IN PARENTHESES.

"I REALLY take it very kind,
This visit, Mrs. Skinner!
I have not seen you such an age —
(The wretch has come to dinner!)

"Your daughters, too, what loves of girls —
What heads for painters' easels!
Come here and kiss the infant, dears, —
(And give it p'r'aps the measles!)

"Your charming boys I see are home
From Reverend Mr. Russell's;
'Twas very kind to bring them both, —
(What boots for my new Brussels!)

"What! little Clara left at home?
Well now I call that shabby:
I should have loved to kiss her so, —
(A flabby, dabby, babby!)

"And Mr. S., I hope he 's well,
Ah! though he lives so handy,

He never now drops in to sup,—
(The better for our brandy!)

"Come, take a seat—I long to hear
About Matilda's marriage;
You're come of course to spend the day!—
(Thank Heaven, I hear the carriage!)

"What! must you go? next time I hope
You'll give me longer measure;
Nay—I shall see you down the stairs—
(With most uncommon pleasure!)

"Good-bye! good-bye! remember all,
Next time you'll take your dinners!
(Now, David, mind I'm not at home
In future to the Skinners!")

EPIGRAMS.

COMPOSED ON READING A DIARY LATELY PUBLISHED.

THAT flesh is grass is now as clear as day,
To any but the merest purblind pup,
Death cuts it down, and then, to make her hay,
My Lady Bury comes and rakes it up.

THE LAST WISH.

When I resign this world so briary,
To have across the Styx my ferrying,
O, may I die without a DIARY !
And be interred without a Bury-ing !

The poor dear dead have been laid out in vain,
Turned into cash, they are laid out again !

THE DEVIL'S ALBUM.

It will seem an odd whim
For a Spirit so grim
As the Devil to take a delight in ;
But by common renown
He has come up to town,
With an Album for people to write in !

On a handsomer book
Mortal never did look,
Of a flame-colour silk is the binding,
With a border superb,
Where through flow'ret and herb,
The old Serpent goes brilliantly winding !

By gilded grotesques,
And embossed arabesques,
The whole cover, in fact, is pervaded;
But, alas! in a taste
That betrays they were traced
At the will of a Spirit degraded!

As for paper — the best,
But extremely hot-pressed,
Courts the pen to luxuriate upon it,
And against every blank
There 's a note on the Bank,
As a bribe for a sketch or a sonnet.

Who will care to appear
In the Fiend's Souvenir,
Is a question to morals most vital;
But the very first leaf,
It 's the public belief,
Will be filled by a Lady of Title!

EPIGRAM.

THE SUPERIORITY OF MACHINERY,

A Mechanic his labor will often discard
If the rate of his pay he dislikes;
But a clock — and its *case* is uncommonly hard—
Will continue to work though it *strikes*.

JOHN DAY.

A PATHETIC BALLAD.

"A Day after the Fair." — OLD PROVERB.

JOHN DAY he was the biggest man
Of all the coachman-kind,
With back too broad to be conceived
By any narrow mind.

The very horses knew his weight
When he was in the rear,
And wished his box a Christmas-box
To come but once a year.

Alas! against the shafts of love,
What armour can avail?
Soon Cupid sent an arrow through
His scarlet coat of mail.

The bar-maid of the Crown he loved,
From whom he never ranged,
For tho' he changed his horses there,
His love he never changed.

He thought her fairest of all fares,
So fondly love prefers;
And often, among twelve outsides,
Deemed no outside like hers.

One day as she was sitting down
Beside the porter-pump —
He came, and knelt with all his fat,
And made an offer plump.

Said she, my taste will never learn
To like so huge a man,
So I must beg you will come here
As little as you can.

But still he stoutly urged his suit,
With vows, and sighs, and tears,
Yet could not pierce her heart, altho'
He drove the Dart for years.

In vain he wooed, in vain he sued;
The maid was cold and proud,
And sent him off to Coventry,
While on his way to Stroud.

He fretted all the way to Stroud,
And thence all back to town,
The course of love was never smooth,
So his went up and down.

At last her coldness made him pine
  To merely bones and skin;
But still he loved like one resolved
  To love through thick and thin.

O Mary, view my wasted back,
  And see my dwindled calf;
Tho' I have never had a wife,
  I've lost my better half.

Alas! in vain he still assailed,
  Her heart withstood the dint;
Though he had carried sixteen stone
  He could not move a flint.

Worn out, at last he made a vow
  To break his being's link;
For he was so reduced in size
  At nothing he could shrink.

Now some will talk in water's praise,
  And waste a deal of breath,
But John, tho' he drank nothing else —
  He drank himself to death.

The cruel maid that caused his love,
  Found out the fatal close,
For looking in the butt, she saw,
  The butt-end of his woes.

Some say his spirit haunts the Crown,
  But that is only talk —
For after riding all his life,
  His ghost objects to walk.

NUMBER ONE.

VERSIFIED FROM THE PROSE OF A YOUNG LADY.

It's very hard! — and so it is,
To live in such a row, —
And witness this that every Miss
But me, has got a Beau. —
For Love goes calling up and down,
But here he seems to shun;
I'm sure he has been asked enough
To call at Number One!

I'm sick of all the double knocks
That come to Number Four! —
At Number Three, I often see
A lover at the door; —
And one in blue, at Number Two,
Calls daily like a dun, —
It's very hard they come so near
And not to Number One!

Miss Bell I hear has got a dear
Exactly to her mind, —
By sitting at the window pane
Without a bit of blind; —
But I go in the balcony,
Which she has never done,
Yet arts that thrive at Number Five
Don't take at Number One!

'Tis hard with plenty in the street,
And plenty passing by, —
There 's nice young men at Number Ten,
But only rather shy; —
And Mrs. Smith across the way
Has got a grown-up son,
But la! he hardly seems to know
There is a Number One!

There 's Mr. Wick at Number Nine
But he 's intent on pelf,
And though he 's pious will not love
His neighbour as himself. —
At Number Seven there was a sale —
The goods had quite a run!
And here I've got my single lot
On hand at Number One!

My mother often sits at work
And talks of props and stays,
And what a comfort I shall be
In her declining days: —

The very maids about the house
Have set me down a nun,
The sweethearts all belong to them
That call at Number One!

Once only when the flue took fire,
One Friday afternoon,
Young Mr. Long came kindly in
And told me not to swoon:—
Why can't he come again without
The Phœnix and the Sun!—
We cannot always have a flue
On fire at Number One!

I am not old! I am not plain!
Nor awkward in my gait—
I am not crooked, like the bride
That went from Number Eight:—
I'm sure white satin made her look
As brown as any bun—
But even beauty has no chance,
I think, at Number One!

At Number Six they say Miss Rose
Has slain a score of hearts,
And Cupid, for her sake, has been
Quite prodigal of darts.
The Imp they show with bended bow,
I wish he had a gun!—
But if he had, he'd never deign
To shoot with Number One.

It 's very hard, and so it is
To live in such a row!
And here 's a ballad singer come
To aggravate my woe; —
O take away your foolish song
And tones enough to stun —
There is "Nae luck about the house,"
I know, at Number One!

THE DROWNING DUCKS.

Amongst the sights that Mrs. Bond
Enjoyed yet grieved at more than others,
Were little ducklings in a pond,
Swimming about beside their mothers —
Small things like living water lilies,
But yellow as the daffo-*dillies*.

"It 's very hard," she used to moan,
"That other people have their ducklings
To grace their waters — mine alone
Have never any pretty chucklings."
For why! — each little yellow navy
Went down — all downy — to old Davy!

She had a lake — a pond I mean —
Its wave was rather thick than pearly —

She had two ducks, their napes were green —
  She had a drake, his tail was curly, —
Yet spite of drake, and ducks, and pond,
No little ducks had Mrs. Bond!

The birds were both the best of mothers —
  The nests had eggs — the eggs had luck —
The infant D.'s came forth like others —
  But there, alas! the matter stuck!
They might as well have all died addle,
As die when they began to paddle! —

For when, as native instinct taught her,
  The mother set her brood afloat,
They sank ere long right under water,
  Like any over-loaded boat;
They were web-footed too to see,
As ducks and spiders ought to be!

No peccant humour in a gander
  Brought havoc on her little folks, —
No poaching cook — a frying pander
  To appetite, — destroyed their yolks, —
Beneath her very eyes, Od' rot 'em!
They went, like plummets, to the bottom.

The thing was strange — a contradiction
  It seemed of nature and her works!
For little ducks, beyond conviction,
  Should float without the help of corks:

Great Johnson it bewildered him!
To hear of ducks that could not swim.

Poor Mrs. Bond! what could she do
But change the breed — and she tried divers
Which dived as all seemed born to do;
No little ones were e'er survivors —
Like those that copy gems, I'm thinking,
They all were given to die-sinking!

In vain their downy coats were shorn; [went!
They floundered still! — Batch after batch
The little fools seemed only born
And hatched for nothing but a hatchment!
Whene'er they launched — O sight of wonder!
Like fires the water "got them under!"

No woman ever gave their lucks
A better chance than Mrs. Bond did;
At last quite out of heart and ducks,
She gave her pond up, and desponded;
For Death among the water-lilies,
Cried "*Duc* ad me" to all her dillies!

But though resolved to breed no more,
She brooded often on this riddle —
Alas! 'twas darker than before!
At last about the summer's middle,
What Johnson, Mrs. Bond, or none did,
To clear the matter up the Sun did!

The thirsty Sirius, dog-like drank
  So deep, his furious tongue to cool,
The shallow waters sank and sank,
  And lo, from out the wasted pool,
Too hot to hold them any longer,
There crawled some eels as big as conger!

I wish all folks would look a bit,
  In such a case below the surface;
But when the eels were caught and split
  By Mrs. Bond, just think of *her* face,
In each inside at once to spy
A duckling turned to giblet-pie!

The sight at once explained the case,
  Making the Dame look rather silly,
The tenants of that *Eely Place*
  Had found the way to *Pick a dilly*,
And so by under-water suction,
Had wrought the little ducks' abduction.

SALLY SIMPKIN'S LAMENT;

OR, JOHN JONES'S KIT-CÀT-ASTROPHE.

"He left his body to the sea,
And made a shark his legatee."
BRYAN AND PERENNE.

"OH! what is that comes gliding in,
And quite in middling haste?
It is the picture of my Jones,
And painted to the waist.

"It is not painted to the life,
For where's the trowsers blue?
O Jones, my dear! — O dear! my Jones,
What is become of you?"

Oh! Sally dear, it is too true,—
The half that you remark
Is come to say my other half
Is bit off by a shark!

Oh! Sally, sharks do things by halves,
Yet most completely do!
A bite in one place seems enough,
But I've been bit in two.

" You know I once was all your own
  But now a shark must share!
But let that pass — for now to you
  I 'm neither here nor there.

" Alas! death has a strange divorce
  Effected in the sea,
It has divided me from you,
  And even me from me!

" Don't fear my ghost will walk o'nights
  To haunt, as people say!
My ghost *can't* walk, for, oh! my legs
  Are many leagues away!

" Lord! think when I am swimming round,
  And looking where the boat is,
A shark just snaps away a *half*,
  Without 'a *quarter's* notice.'

" One half is here, the other half
  Is near Columbia placed;
Oh! Sally, I have got the whole
  Atlantic for my waist.

" But now, adieu — a long adieu!
  I 've solved death's awful riddle,
And would say more, but I am doomed
  To break off in the middle!"

THE FALL.

"Down, down, down, ten thousand fathoms deep."
COUNT FATHOM.

WHO does not know that dreadful gulf, where Niagara falls,
Where eagle unto eagle screams, to vulture vulture calls;
Where down beneath, Despair and Death in liquid darkness grope,
And upward, on the foam there shines a rainbow without Hope;
While, hung with clouds of Fear and Doubt, the unreturning wave
Suddenly gives an awful plunge, like life into the grave;
And many a hapless mortal there hath dived to bale or bliss;
One — only one — hath ever lived to rise from that abyss!
Oh, Heaven! it turns me now to ice with chill of fear extreme,
To think of my frail bark adrift on that tumultuous stream!
In vain with desperate sinews, strung by love of life and light,

I urged that coffin, my canoe, against the current's
might:
On — on — still on — direct for doom, the river
rushed in force,
And fearfully the stream of Time raced with it in
its course.
My eyes I closed — I dared not look the way
towards the goal;
But still I viewed the horrid close, and dreamt it
in my soul.
Plainly, as through transparent lids, I saw the
fleeting shore,
And lofty trees, like winged things, flit by for
evermore;
Plainly — but with no prophet sense — I heard
the sullen sound,
The torrent's voice — and felt the mist, like death-
sweat gathering round.
O agony! O life! My home! and those that
made it sweet:
Ere I could pray, the torrent lay beneath my
very feet.
With frightful whirl, more swift than thought, I
passed the dizzy edge,
Bound after bound, with hideous bruise, I dashed
from ledge to ledge,
From crag to crag — in speechless pain — from
midnight deep to deep;
I did not die — but anguish stunned my senses
into sleep.

How long entranced, or whither dived, no clue I
have to find:
At last the gradual light of life came dawning
o'er my mind;
And through my brain there thrilled a cry — a
cry as shrill as birds'
Of vulture or of eagle kind, but this was set to
words: —
"It's Edgar Huntley in his cap and nightgown, I
declares!
He's been a walking in his sleep, and pitched all
down the stairs!"

STEAM SEA SONGS.

I STEAMED from the Downs in the Nancy,
My jib how she *smoked* through the breeze
She's a vessel as tight to my fancy
As ever *boiled* through the salt seas.

*   *   *   *

When up the *flue* the sailor goes
And ventures on the *pot*,
The landsman, he no better knows,
But thinks hard is his lot.

Bold Jack with smiles each danger meets,
Weighs anchor, lights the log;

Trims up the fire, picks out the slates,
And drinks his can of grog
* * * *

Go patter to lubbers and swabs do you see,
'Bout danger, and fear, and the like;
But a *Boulton and Watt* and good *Wall's-end* give me;
And it ain't to a little I 'll strike.

Though the tempest our *chimney* smack smooth shall down smite,
And shiver each *bundle* of wood;
Clear the wreck, *stir the fire*, and stow every thing tight,
And *boiling a gallop* we'll scud.
* * * *

Hark, the boatswain hoarsely bawling,
By shovel, tongs, and poker, stand;
Down the scuttle quick be hauling,
Down your bellows, hand, boys, hand.
Now it freshens —blow like blazes;
Now unto the coal-hole go;
Stir, boys, stir, don't mind black faces,
Up your ashes nimbly throw.

Ply your bellows, raise the wind, boys,
See the valve is clear of course;
Let the paddles spin, don't mind, boys,
Though the weather should be worse.
Fore and aft a proper draft get,

Oil the engines, see all clear;
Hands up, each a sack of coal get,
Man the boiler, cheer, lads, cheer;
Now the dreadful thunder 's roaring,
Peal on peal contending clash;
On our heads fierce rain falls pouring,
In our eyes the paddles splash.
One wide water all around us,
All above one smoke-black sky:
Different deaths at once surround us;
Hark! what means that dreadful cry.

The funnel 's gone! cries every tongue out,
The engineer 's washed off the deck;
A leak beneath the coal-hole 's sprung out,
Call all hands to clear the wreck.
Quick, some coal, some nubbly pieces;
Come, my hearts, be stout and bold;
Plumb the boiler, speed decreases,
Four feet water getting cold.

While o'er the ship wild waves are beating,
We for wives or children mourn;
Alas! from hence there 's no retreating;
Alas! to them there 's no return.
The fire is out — we 've burst the bellows,
The tinder-box is swamped below;
Heaven have mercy on poor fellows,
For only that can serve us now!

A LAY OF REAL LIFE.

"Some are born with a wooden spoon in their mouths, and some with a golden ladle." — GOLDSMITH.

"Some are born with tin rings in their noses, and some with silver ones." — SILVERSMITH.

WHO ruined me ere I was born,
Sold every acre, grass or corn,
And left the next heir all forlorn
My Grandfather.

Who said my motner was no nurse,
And physicked me and made me worse,
Till infancy became a curse?
My Grandmother.

Who left me in my seventh year,
A comfort to my mother dear,
And Mr. Pope, the overseer?
My Father.

Who let me starve, to buy her gin,
Till all my bones came through my skin,
Then called me "ugly little sin?"
My Mother.

Who said my mother was a Turk
And took me home — and made me work,
But managed half my meals to shirk?
My Aunt.

Who "of all earthly things" would boast,
"He hated others' brats the most,"
And therefore made me feel my post?
My Uncle.

Who got in scrapes, an endless score,
And always laid them at my door,
Till many a bitter bang I bore?
My Cousin.

Who took me home when mother died,
Again with father to reside,
Black shoes, clean knives, run far and wide?
My Stepmother.

Who marred my stealthy urchin joys,
And when I played cried "What a noise!" —
Girls always hector over boys —
My Sister.

Who used to share in what was mine,
Or took it all, did he incline,
'Cause I was eight, and he was nine?
My Brother.

Who stroked my head, and said " Good lad,"
And gave me sixpence, " all he had ; "
But at the stall the coin was bad ?
My Godfather.

Who, gratis, shared my social glass,
But when misfortune came to pass,
Referred me to the pump ? Alas !
My Friend.

Through all this weary world, in brief,
Who ever sympathized with grief,
Or shared my joy — my sole relief ?
Myself.

A VALENTINE.

THE WEATHER TO P. MURPHY,* ESQ., M.N.S.

These, properly speaking, being esteemed the three arms of Meteoric action.

DEAR Murphy, to improve her charms,
Your servant humbly begs ;
She thanks you for her leash of arms,
But wants a brace of legs.

* An Almanac-maker.

Moreover, as you promise folks,
  On certain days a drizzle ;
She thinks, in case she cannot rain,
  She should have means to *mizzle.*

Some lightning too may just fall due,
  When woods begin to moult ;
And if she cannot "fork it out,"
  She 'll wish to make a *bolt !*

POEM — FROM THE POLISH.

Some months since a young lady was much surprised at receiving, from the Captain of a Whaler, a blank sheet of paper, folded in the form of a letter, and duly sealed. At last, recollecting the nature of sympathetic ink, she placed the missive on a toasting-fork, and after holding it to the fire for a minute or two, succeeded in thawing out the following verses.

FROM seventy-two north latitude,
  Dear Kitty, I indite ;
But first I'd have you understand
  How hard it is to write.

Of thoughts that breathe and words that [burn,
  My Kitty, do not think,—
Before I wrote these very lines,
  I had to melt my ink.

Of mutual flames and lovers' warmth,
 You must not be too nice;
The sheet that I am writing on
 Was once a sheet of ice!

The Polar cold is sharp enough
 To freeze with icy gloss
The genial current of the soul,
 E'en in a "Man of Ross."

Pope says that letters waft a sigh
 From Indus to the Pole;
But here I really wish the post
 Would only "post the *coal.*"

So chilly is the Northern blast,
 It blows me through and through;
A ton of Wallsend in a note
 Would be a billet-doux!

In such a frigid latitude
 It scarce can be a sin,
Should Passion cool a little, where
 A Fury was iced in.

I'm rather tired of endless snow,
 And long for coals again;
And would give up a Sea of Ice,
 For some of Lambton's Main.

I 'm sick of dazzling ice and snow,
  The sun itself I hate;
So very bright, so very cold,
  Just like a summer grate.

For opodeldoc I would kneel,
  My chilblains to anoint;
O Kate, the needle of the north
  Has got a freezing point.

Our food *is* solids,— ere we put
  Our meat into our crops,
We take sledge-hammers to our steaks
  And hatchets to our chops.

So very bitter is the blast,
  So cutting is the air,
I never have been warm but once,
  When hugging with a bear.

One thing I know you 'll like to hear,
  The effect of Polar snows,
I 've left off snuff — one pinching day —
  From leaving off my nose.

I have no ear for music now;
  My ears both left together;
And as for dancing, I have cut
  My toes — it 's cutting weather.

I 've said that you should have my hand,
Some happy day to come;
But, Kate, you only now can wed
A finger and a thumb.

Don't fear that any Esquimaux
Can wean me from my own;
The Girdle of the Queen of Love
Is not the Frozen Zone.

At wives with large estates of snow
My fancy does not bite;
I like to see a Bride — but not
In such a deal of white.

Give me for home a house of brick,
The Kate I love at Kew!
A hand unchopped — a merry eye,
And not a nose, of blue!

To think upon the Bridge of Kew,
To me a bridge of sighs;
Oh, Kate, a pair of icicles
Are standing in my eyes!

God knows if I shall e'er return,
In comfort to be lulled;
But if I do get back to port,
Pray let me have it mulled.

CONVEYANCING.

O, LONDON is the place for all,
  In love with loco-motion!
Still to and fro the people go
  Like billows of the ocean;
Machine or man, or caravan,
  Can all be had for paying,
When great estates, or heavy weights,
  Or bodies want conveying.

There 's always hacks about in packs,
  Wherein you may be shaken,
And Jarvis is not always *drunk*,
  Tho' always *overtaken;*
In racing tricks he 'll never mix,
  His nags are in their last days,
And *slow* to go, altho' they show
  As if they had their *fast days!*

Then if you like a single horse,
  This age is quite a *cab-age*,
A car not quite so small and light
  As those of our Queen *Mab* age;

The horses have been *broken well,*
All danger is rescinded,
For some have *broken both their knees*
And some are *broken winded.*

If you 've a friend at Chelsea end,
The stages are worth knowing —
There is a sort, we call 'em short,
Although the longest going —
For some will stop at Hatchett's shop,
Till you grow faint and sicky,
Perched up behind, at last to find,
Your dinner is all *dickey!*

Lon stages run from every yard;
But if you 're wise and frugal,
You 'll never go with any Guard
That plays upon the bugle,
"Ye banks and braes," and other lays,
And ditties everlasting,
Like miners going all your way,
With *boring* and with *blasting.*

Instead of *journeys,* people now
May go upon a *Gurney,*
With steam to do the horses' work,
By *powers of attorney;*
Tho' with a load it may explode,
And you may all be *un*-done!
And find you 're going *up to Heaven,*
Instead of *up to London!*

To speak of every kind of coach,
It is not my intention ;
But there is still one vehicle
Deserves a little mention ;
The world a sage has called a stage,
With all its living lumber,
And Malthus swears it always bears
Above the proper number.

The law will transfer house or land
Forever and a day hence,
For lighter things, watch, brooches, rings,
You 'll never want conveyance ;
Ho ! stop the thief ! my handkerchief !
It is no sight for laughter —
Away it goes, and leaves my nose
To join in running after !

EPICUREAN REMINISCENCES OF A SENTIMENTALIST.

"My *Tables!* *Meat* it is, *I set it* down!" — HAMLET.

I THINK it was Spring — but not certain I am —
When my passion began first to work ;
But I know we were certainly looking for lamb,
And the season was over for pork.

'Twas at Christmas, I think, when I met with Miss Chase,
Yes,— for Morris had asked me to dine,—
And I thought I had never beheld such a face,
Or so noble a turkey and chine.

Placed close by her side, it made others quite [wild,
With sheer envy to witness my luck;
How she blushed as I gave her some turtle, and smiled
As I afterwards offered some duck.

I looked and I languished, alas, to my cost,
Through three courses of dishes and meats;
Getting deeper in love — but my heart was quite lost,
When it came to the trifle and sweets!

With a rent-roll that told of my houses and land,
To her parents I told my designs —
And then to herself I presented my hand,
With a very fine pottle of pines!

I asked her to have me for weal or for woe,
And she did not object in the least; —
I can't tell the date — but we married, I know,
Just in time to have game at the feast.

We went to ———, it certainly was the seaside;
For the next, the most blessed of morns,

I remember how fondly I gazed at my bride,
  Sitting down to a plateful of prawns.

O never may memory lose sight of that year,
  But still hallow the time as it ought,
That season the "grass" was remarkably dear,
  And the peas at a guinea a quart.

So happy, like hours, all our days seemed to haste,
  A fond pair, such as poets have drawn,
So united in heart — so congenial in taste,
  We were both of us partial to brawn!

A long life I looked for of bliss with my bride,
  But then Death — I ne'er dreamt about that!
Oh there 's nothing is certain in life, as I cried,
  When my turbot eloped with the cat!

My dearest took ill at the turn of the year,
  But the cause no physician could nab;
But something it seemed like consumption, I fear,
  It was just after supping on crab.

In vain she was doctored, in vain she was dosed,
  Still her strength and her appetite pined;
She lost relish for what she had relished the most,
  Even salmon she deeply declined.

For months still I lingered in hope and in doubt,
  While her form it grew wasted and thin;

But the last dying spark of existence went out,
As the oysters were just coming in!

She died, and she left me the saddest of men
To indulge in a widower's moan,
Oh, I felt all the power of solitude then,
As I ate my first natives alone!

But when I beheld Virtue's friends in their cloaks,
And with sorrowful crape on their hats,
O my grief poured a flood! and the out-of-door folks
Were all crying — I think it was sprats!

I'M NOT A SINGLE MAN.

"Double, single, and the rub." — Hoyle.
"This, this is Solitude." — Byron.

I.

Well, I confess, I did not guess
A simple marriage vow
Would make me find all women-kind
Such unkind women now!
They need not, sure, as *distant* be
As Java or Japan,—
Yet every Miss reminds me this —
I'm not a single man!

II.

Once they made choice of my bass voice
To share in each duet;
So well I danced, I somehow chanced
To stand in every set:
They now declare I cannot sing,
And dance on Bruin's plan;
Me draw — me paint! — me any thing! —
I'm not a single man!

III.

Once I was asked advice, and tasked
What works to buy or not,
And "would I read that passage out
I so admired in Scott?"
They then could bear to hear one read;
But if I now began,
How they would snub, "My pretty page,"
I'm not a single man!

IV.

One used to stitch a collar then,
Another hemmed a frill;
I had more purses netted then
Than I could hope to fill.
I once could get a button on,
But now I never can —
My buttons then were Bachelor's —
I'm not a single man!

V.

Oh how they hated politics
  Thrust on me by papa:
But now my chat — they all leave that
  To entertain mamma.
Mamma, who praises her own self,
  Instead of Jane or Ann,
And lays "her girls" upon the shelf —
  I'm not a single man!

VI.

Ah me, how strange it is the change,
  In parlour and in hall,
They treat me so, if I but go
  To make a morning call.
If they had hair in papers once,
  Bolt up the stairs they ran;
They now sit still in dishabille —
  I'm not a single man!

VII.

Miss Mary Bond was once so fond
  Of Romans and of Greeks;
She daily sought my cabinet,
  To study my antiques.
Well, now she doesn't care a dump
  For ancient pot or pan,
Her taste at once is modernized —
  I'm not a single man!

VIII.

My spouse is fond of homely life,
  And all that sort of thing;
I go to balls without my wife,
  And never wear a ring:
And yet each Miss to whom I come,
  As strange as Genghis Khan,
Knows by some sign, I can't divine —
  I'm not a single man!

IX.

Go where I will, I but intrude,
  I'm left in crowded rooms,
Like Zimmerman on Solitude,
  Or Hervey at his Tombs.
From head to heel, they make me feel,
  Of quite another clan;
Compelled to own, though left alone —
  I'm not a single man!

X.

Miss Towne the toast, though she can boast
  A nose of Roman line,
Will turn up even that in scorn
  Of compliments of mine:
She should have seen that I have been
  Her sex's partisan,
And really married all I could —
  I'm not a single man!

XI.

'Tis hard to see how others fare,
  Whilst I rejected stand,—
Will no one take my arm because
  They cannot have my hand?
Miss Parry, that for some would go
  A trip to Hindostan,
With me don't care to mount a stair—
  I 'm not a single man!

XII.

Some change, of course, should be in force,
  But, surely, not so much —
There may be hands I may not squeeze,
  But must I never touch? —
Must I forbear to hand a chair
  And not pick up a fan?
But I have been myself picked up —
  I 'm not a single man!

XIII.

Others may hint a lady's tint
  Is purest red and white —
May say her eyes are like the skies,
  So very blue and bright,—
I must not say that she *has eyes*,
  Or if I so began,
I have my fears about my ears —
  I 'm not a single man!

XIV.

I must confess I did not guess
A simple marriage vow,
Would make me find all women-kind
Such unkind women now ; —
I might be hashed to death, or smashed,
By Mr. Pickford's van,
Without, I fear, a single tear —
I 'm not a single man !

THE BURNING OF THE LOVE-LETTER.

"Sometimes they were put to the proof, by what was called the Fiery Ordeal." — HIST. ENG.

No morning ever seemed so long ! —
I tried to read with all my might !
In my left hand "My Landlord's Tales,"
And threepence ready in my right.

'Twas twelve at last — my heart beat high ! —
The Postman rattled at the door ! —
And just upon her road to church,
I dropt the "Bride of Lammermoor !"

I seized the note — I flew up stairs —
Flung-to the door, and locked me in —
With panting haste I tore the seal —
And kissed the B in Benjamin!

'Twas full of love — to rhyme with dove —
And all that tender sort of thing —
Of sweet and meet — and heart and dart —
But not a word about a ring! —

In doubt I cast it in the flame,
And stood to watch the latest spark —
And saw the love all end in smoke —
Without a Parson and a Clerk!

THE APPARITION.

In the dead of the night, when, from beds that
  are turfy,
The spirits rise up on old cronies to call,
Came a shade from the Shades on a visit to
  Murphy,
Who had not foreseen such a visit at all.

Don't shiver and shake, said the mild Apparition,
I'm come to your bed with no evil design;

I 'm the Spirit of Moore, Francis Moore the
Physician,
Once great like yourself in the Almanac line.

Like you I was once a great prophet on weather,
And deemed to possess a more prescient knack
Than dogs, frogs, pigs, cattle, or cats, all together,
The donkeys that bray, and the dillies that quack.

With joy, then, as ashes retain former passion,
I saw my old mantle lugged out from the shelf,
Turned, trimmed, and brushed up, and again
brought in fashion,
I seemed to be almost reviving myself!

But, oh! from my joys there was soon a sad
cantle —
As too many cooks make a mull of the broth —
To find that two Prophets were under my mantle,
And pulling two ways at the risk of the cloth.

Unless you would meet with an awkwardish
tumble,
Oh! join like the Siamese twins in your jumps;
Just fancy if Faith on her Prophets should stumble,
The one in his clogs, and the other in pumps!

But think how the people would worship and
wonder,
To find you "hail fellows, well met," in your hail,

In one tune with your rain, and your wind, and
your thunder,
"'Fore God," they would cry, "they are both in
a tale!"

LITTLE O'P.—AN AFRICAN FACT.

It was July the First, and the great hill of Howth
Was bearing by compass sow-west and by south,
And the name of the ship was the Peggy of Cork,
Well freighted with bacon and butter and pork.
Now, this ship had a captain, Macmorris by name,
And little O'Patrick was mate of the same;
For Bristol they sailed, but by nautical scope,
They contrived to be lost by the Cape of Good
Hope.
Of all the Cork boys that the vessel could boast,
Only little O'P. made a swim to the coast;
And when he revived from a sort of a trance,
He saw a big Black with a very long lance.
Says the savage, says he, in some Hottentot
tongue,
"Bash Kuku my gimmel bo gumborry bung!"
Then blew a long shell, to the fright of our elf,
And down came a hundred as black as himself.
They brought with them *guattul*, and pieces of
klam,

The first was like beef, and the second like lamb;
"Don't I know," said O'P., "what the wretches
are at?
They're intending to eat me as soon as I'm fat!"
In terror of coming to pan, spit, or pot,
His rations of *jarbul* he suffered to rot;
He would not touch *purry* or *doolberry-lik*,
But kept himself *growing* as thin as a stick.
Though broiling the climate, and parching with
drouth,
He would not let *chobbery* enter his mouth,
But kicked down the *krug* shell, tho' sweetened
with *natt*,—
"I ain't to be pisoned the likes of a rat!"
At last the great *Joddry* got quite in a rage,
And cried, "O mi pitticum dambally nage!
The *chobbery* take, and put back on the shelf,
Or give me the *krug* shell, I'll drink it myself!
The *doolberry-lik* is the best to be had,
And the *purry* (I chewed it myself) is not bad;
The *jarbul* is fresh, for I saw it cut out,
And the *Bok* that it came from is grazing about.
My *jumbo!* but run off to Billery Nang,
And tell her to put on her *jigger* and *tang*,
And go with the *Bloss* to the man of the sea,
And say that she comes as his *Wulwul* from me."
Now Billery Nang was as Black as a sweep,
With thick curly hair like the wool of a sheep,
And the moment he spied her, said little O'P.,
"Sure the Divil is dead, and his Widow 's at me!"

But when, in the blaze of her Hottentot-charms,
She came to accept him for life in her arms,
And stretched her thick lips to a broad grin of
love,
A Raven preparing to bill like a Dove,
With a soul full of dread he declined the grim
bliss,
Stopped her Molyneux arms, and eluded her
kiss;
At last, fairly foiled, she gave up the attack,
And *Joddry* began to look blacker than black;
"By Mumbo! by Jumbo! — why here is a man,
That won't be made happy do all that I can;
He will not be married, lodged, clad, and well fed,
Let the *Rham* take his *shangwang* and chop off
his head!"

THE ANGLER'S FAREWELL.

"Resigned, I kissed the rod."

WELL! I think it is time to put up!
For it does not accord with my notions,
Wrist, elbow, and chine,
Stiff from throwing the line,
To take nothing at last by my motions!

I ground-bait my way as I go,
And dip in at each watery dimple;
  But however I wish
  To inveigle the fish,
To my *gentle* they will not play *simple!*

Though my float goes so swimmingly on,
My bad luck never seems to diminish;
  It would seem that the Bream
  Must be scarce in the stream,
And the *Chub*, tho' it's chubby, be *thinnish!*

Not a Trout there can be in the place,
Not a Grayling or Rud worth the mention,
  And although at my hook
  With *attention* I look,
I can ne'er see my hook with *a Tench on!*

At a brandling once Gudgeon would gape,
But they seem upon different terms now;
  Have they taken advice
  Of the "*Council of Nice*,"
And rejected their "*Diet of Worms*," now?

In vain my live minnow I spin,
Not a Pike seems to think it worth snatching;
  For the gut I have brought,
  I had better have bought
A good *rope* that was used to *Jack-ketching!*

Not a nibble has ruffled my cork,
It is vain in this river to search then ;
  I may wait till it 's night,
  Without any bite,
And at *roost-time* have never a *Perch* then !

No Roach can I meet with — no Bleak,
Save what in the air is so sharp now ;
  Not a Dace have I got,
  And I fear it is not
" Carpe diem," a day for the Carp now !

Oh ! there is not a one pound prize
To be got in this fresh water-lottery !
  What then can I deem
  Of so fishless a stream
But that 'tis — like St. Mary's — *Ottery !*

For an Eel I have learned how to try,
By a method of Walton's own showing,—
  But a fisherman feels
  Little prospect of Eels,
In a path that 's devoted to towing !

I have tried all the water for miles,
Till I 'm weary of dipping and casting,
  And hungry and faint,—
  Let the Fancy just paint
What it is, *without Fish*, to be *Fasting !*

And the rain drizzles down very fast,
While my dinner-time sounds from a far bell,—
  So, wet to the skin,
  I 'll e'en back to my Inn,
Where at least I am sure of a *Bar-bell!*

SEA SONG.

AFTER DIBDIN.

PURE water it plays a good part in
The swabbing the decks and all that —
And it finds its own level for sartin —
For it sartinly drinks very flat: —
For my part a drop of the creatur
I never could think was a fault,
For if Tars should swig water by natur,
The sea would have never been salt! —
Then off with it into a jorum
And make it strong, sharpish, or sweet,
For if I 've any sense of decorum
It never was meant to be neat! —

One day when I was but half sober,—
Half measures I always disdain —
I walked into a shop that sold Soda,
And axed for some Water Champagne: —

Well, the lubber he drew and he drew, boys,
Till I 'd shipped my six bottles or more,
And blow off my last limb but it 's true, boys
Why, I warn't half so drunk as afore! —
Then off with it into a jorum,
And make it strong, sharpish, or sweet,
For if I 've any sense of decorum,
It never was meant to be neat.

STANZAS ON COMING OF AGE.

" Twiddle'em, Twaddle'em, Twenty-one."

Nurse. O woe! O woeful, woeful, woeful day!
Most lamentable day! most woeful day!
That ever, ever, I did yet behold!
O day! O day! O day! O hateful day!
Never was seen so black a day as this!
O woeful day! O woeful day!

* * * *

Musician. Faith, we may put up our pipes and be gone.
Nurse. Honest good fellows, ah! put up, put up!
For well you know this is a pitiful case.

ROMEO AND JULIET.

TO-DAY it is my natal day,
Three 'prenticeships have passed away,
A part in work, a part in play,
  Since I was bound to life!
This first of May I come of age,

A man, I enter on the stage
Where human passions fret and rage,
To mingle in the strife.

It ought to be a happy date,
My friends, they all congratulate
That I am come to "Man's Estate,"
To some, a grand event;
But ah! to me descent allots
No acres, no paternal spots
In Beds, Bucks, Herts, Wilts, Essex, Notts,
Hants, Oxon, Berks, or Kent.

From John o'Groat's to Land's End search,
I have not one rod, pole, or perch,
To pay my rent, or tithe to church,
That I can call my own.
Not common-right for goose or ass;
Then what is Man's Estate? Alas!
Six feet by two of mould and grass
When I am dust and bone.

Reserve the feast! The board forsake!
Ne'er tap the wine—don't cut the cake,
No toasts or foolish speeches make,
At which my reason spurns.
Before this happy term you praise,
And prate about returns and days,
Just o'er my vacant rent-roll gaze,
And sum up my returns.

I know where great estates descend
That here is Boyhood's legal end,
And easily can comprehend
  How "Manors make the Man."
But as for me, I was not born
To quitrent of a peppercorn,
And gain no ground this blessed morn
  From Beersheba to Dan.

No barrels broach — no bonfires make!
To roast a bullock for my sake,
Who in the country have no stake,
  Would be too like a quiz;
No banners hoist — let off no gun —
Pitch no marquee — devise no fun —
But think when man is Twenty-One
  What new delights are his!

What is the moral legal fact —
Of age to day, I 'm free to act
For self — free, namely, to contract
  Engagements, bonds, and debts;
I 'm free to give my I O U,
Sign, draw, accept, as majors do;
And free to lose my freedom too
  For want of due assets.

I am of age, to ask Miss Ball,
Or that great heiress, Miss Duval,
To go to church, hump, squint, and all,

And be my own for life.
But put such reasons on their shelves,
To tell the truth between ourselves,
I 'm one of those contented elves
Who do not want a wife.

What else belongs to Manhood still?
I 'm old enough to make my will
With valid clause and codicil
Before in turf I lie.
But I have nothing to bequeathe
In earth, or waters underneath,
And in all candour let me breathe,
I do not want to die.

Away! if this be Manhood's forte,
Put by the sherry and the port —
No ring of bells — no rustic sport —
No dance — no merry pipes!
No flowery garlands — no bouquet —
No Birthday Ode to sing or say —
To me it seems this is a day
For bread and cheese and swipes.

To justify the festive cup
What horrors here are conjured up!
What things of bitter bite and sup,
Poor wretched Twenty-One's!
No landed lumps, but frumps and humps,
(Discretion's Days are far from trumps)

Domestic discord, dowdies, dumps,
  Death, dockets, debts, and duns!

If you must drink, oh drink "the King"
Reform — the Church — the Press — the
    Ring,
Drink Aldgate Pump — or any thing,
  Before a toast like this!
Nay, tell me, coming thus of age,
And turning o'er this sorry page,
Was young Nineteen so far from sage?
  Or young Eighteen from bliss?

Till this dull, cold, wet, happy morn —
No sign of May about the thorn,—
Were Love and Bacchus both unborn?
  Had Beauty not a shape?
Make answer, sweet Kate Finnerty!
Make answer, lads of Trinity!
Who sipped with me Divinity,
  And quaffed the ruby grape!

No flummery then from flowery lips,
No three times three and hip-hip-hips,
Because I 'm ripe and full of pips —
  I like a little green.
To put me on my solemn oath,
If sweep-like I could stop my growth
I would remain, and nothing loth,
  A boy — about nineteen.

My friends, excuse me these rebukes!
Were I a monarch's son, or duke's,
Go to the Vatican of Meux
And broach his biggest barrels —
Impale whole elephants on spits —
Ring Tom of Lincoln till he splits,
And dance into St. Vitus' fits,
And break your winds with carols!

But ah! too well you know my lot,
Ancestral acres greet me not,
My freehold's in a garden-pot,
And barely worth a pin.
Away then with all festive stuff!
Let Robins advertise and puff
My "Man's Estate," I'm sure enough
I shall not buy it in.

A SINGULAR EXHIBITION AT SOMERSET HOUSE.

"Our Crummie is a dainty cow." — Scotch Song.

On that first Saturday in May,
When Lords and Ladies, great and grand,
Repair to see what each R. A.
Has done since last they sought the Strand,

In red, brown, yellow, green, or blue,
In short, what 's called the private view,
Amongst the guests — the deuce knows how
She got in there without a row —
There came a large and vulgar dame
With arms deep red, and face the same,
Showing in temper not a Saint;
No one could guess for why she came,
Unless perchance to "scour the Paint."

From wall to wall she forced her way,
Elbowed Lord Durham — poked Lord Grey —
Stamped Stafford's toes to make him move,
And Devonshire's Duke received a shove;
The great Lord Chancellor felt her nudge,
She made the Vice, his Honour, budge,
And gave a pinch to Park the Judge.
As for the ladies, in this stir,
The highest rank gave way to her.
From number one and number two,
She searched the pictures through and through,
On benches stood, to inspect the high ones,
And squatted down to scan the shy ones.
And as she went from part to part,
A deeper red each cheek became,
Her very eyes lit up in flame,
That made each looker-on exclaim,
"Really an ardent love of art!"
Alas, amidst her inquisition,
Fate brought her to a sad condition;

She might have run against Lord Milton,
And still have stared at deeds in oil,
But ah! her picture-joy to spoil,
She came full butt on Mr. Hilton.

The Keeper mute, with staring eyes,
Like a lay-figure for surprise,
At last thus stammered out "How now?
Woman — where, woman, is your ticket,
That ought to let you through our wicket?"
Says woman, "Where is David's Cow?"
Said Mr. H——, with expedition,
There 's no Cow in the Exhibition.
"No Cow!" — but here her tongue in verity,
Set off with steam and rail celerity —

"No Cow! there ain't no Cow, then the more 's the shame and pity
Hang you and the R. A.'s, and all the Hanging Committee!
No Cow — but hold your tongue, for you needn't talk to me —
You can't talk up the Cow, you can't, to where it ought to be —
I have n't seen a picture high or low, or any how,
Or in any of the rooms to be compared with David's Cow?
You may talk of your Landseers, and of your Coopers, and your Wards,

Why hanging is too good for them, and yet here
they are on cords!
They 're only fit for window frames, and shutters,
and street doors,
David will paint 'em any day at Red Lions or
Blue Boars, —
Why Morland was a fool to him, at a little pig or
sow —
It 's really hard it ain't hung up — I could cry
about the Cow!
But I know well what it is, and why — they 're
jealous of David's fame,
But to vent it on the Cow, poor thing, is a cruelty
and a shame.
Do you think it might hang by and by, if you
cannot hang it now?
David has made a party up, to come and see his
Cow.
If it only hung three days a week, for an exam-
ple to the learners,
Why can't it hang up, turn about, with that pic-
ture of Mr. Turner's?
Or do you think from Mr. Etty, you need appre-
hend a row,
If now and then you cut him down to hang up
David's Cow?
I can't think where their tastes have been, to not
have such a creature,
Although I say, that should not say, it was pret-
tier than Nature;

It must be hung — and shall be hung, for Mr.
H——, I vow,
I daren't take home the catalogue, unless it 's got
the Cow!
As we only want it to be seen, I should not so
much care,
If it was only round the stone man's neck, a-com-
ing up the stair.
Or down there in the marble room where all the
figures stand,
Where one of them three Graces might just hold it
in her hand —
Or may be Bailey's Charity the favour would
allow,
It would really be a charity to hang up David's
cow.
We haven't no where else to go if you don't hang
it here,
The Water-Colour place allows no oilman to ap-
pear —
And the British Gallery sticks to Dutch, Teniers,
and Gerrard Douw,
And the Suffolk Gallery will not do — it 's not a
Suffolk Cow:
I wish you 'd seen him painting her, he hardly
took his meals
Till she was painted on the board correct from
head to heels;
His heart and soul was in his Cow, and almost
made him shabby,

He hardly whipped the boys at all, or helped to
nurse the babby.
And when he had her all complete and painted
over red,
He got so grand, I really thought him going off
his head.
Now hang it, Mr. Hilton, do just hang it any
how,
Poor David, he will hang himself, unless you
hang his Cow.—
And if it 's unconvenient and drawn too big by
half —
David shan't send next year except a very little
calf.

I'M GOING TO BOMBAY.

"Nothing venture, nothing have." — Old Proverb.

"Every Indiaman has at least two mates."
Falconer's Marine Guide.

I.

My hair is brown, my eyes are blue,
And reckoned rather bright;
I 'm shapely, if they tell me true,
And just the proper height;
My skin has been admired in verse,

And called as fair as day —
If I *am* fair, so much the worse,
I'm going to Bombay!

II.

At school I passed with some éclât;
I learned my French in France;
De Wint gave lessons how to draw,
And D'Egville how to dance; —
Crevelli taught me how to sing,
And Cramer how to play —
It really is the strangest thing —
I'm going to Bombay!

III.

I 've been to Bath and Cheltenham Wells,
But not their springs to sip —
To Ramsgate — not to pick up shells, —
To Brighton — not to dip.
I 've toured the Lakes, and scoured the coast
From Scarboro' to Torquay —
But tho' of time I 've made the most,
I 'm going to Bombay!

IV.

By Pa and Ma I 'm daily told
To marry now 's my time,
For though I 'm very far from old
I 'm rather in my prime.

They say while we have any sun
We ought to make our hay —
And India has so hot an one,
I 'm going to Bombay !

V.

My cousin writes from Hyderapot
My only chance to snatch,
And says the climate is so hot,
It 's sure to light a match,—
She's married to a son of Mars,
With very handsome pay,
And swears I ought to thank my stars
I 'm going to Bombay !

VI.

She says that I shall much delight
To taste their Indian treats,
But what she likes may turn me quite,
Their strange outlandish meats. —
If I can eat rupees, who knows ?
Or dine, the Indian way,
On doolies and on bungalows —
I 'm going to Bombay !

VII.

She says that I shall much enjoy,—
I don't know what she means, —
To take the air and buy some toy,

In my own palankeens, —
I like to drive my pony-chair,
Or ride our dapple gray —
But elephants are horses there —
I 'm going to Bombay!

VIII.

Farewell, farewell, my parents dear,
My friends, farewell to them!
And oh, what costs a sadder tear,
Good-bye, to Mr. M! —
If I should find an Indian vault,
Or fall a tiger's prey,
Or steep in salt, it 's all *his* fault,
I 'm going to Bombay!

IX.

That fine new teak-built ship, the Fox,
A.I. — Commander Bird,
Now lying in the London Docks,
Will sail on May the Third;
Apply for passage or for freight,
To Nichol, Scott, and Gray —
Pa has applied and sealed my fate —
I 'm going to Bombay!

X.

My heart is full — my trunks as well;
My mind and caps made up,

My corsets shaped by Mrs. Bell,
Are promised ere I sup;
With boots and shoes, Rivarta's best,
And dresses by Ducé,
And a special license in my chest —
I 'm going to Bombay!

ODE

TO THE ADVOCATES FOR THE REMOVAL OF SMITHFIELD MARKET.

"Sweeping our flocks and herds." — DOUGLAS.

O PHILANTHROPIC men! —
For this address I need not make apology —
Who aim at clearing out the Smithfield pen,
And planting further off its vile Zoology —
Permit me thus to tell,
I like your efforts well,
For routing that great nest of Hornithology!

Be not dismayed, although repulsed at first,
And driven from their Horse, and Pig, and Lamb parts,
Charge on! — you shall upon their hornworks burst,
And carry all their *Bull*-warks and their *Ram*-parts,

Go on, ye wholesale drovers!
And drive away the Smithfield flocks and herds!
As wild as Tartar-Curds,
That come so fat, and kicking, from their clovers,
Off with them all! — those restive brutes, that vex
Our streets, and plunge, and lunge, and butt, and
battle;
And save the female sex
From being cowed — like Iö — by the cattle!

Fancy, — when droves appear on
The hill of Holborn, roaring from its top,—
Your ladies — ready, as they own, to drop,
Taking themselves to Thomson's with a *Fear-on!*

Or, in St. Martin's Lane,
Scared by a Bullock, in a frisky vein,—
Fancy the terror of your timid daughters,
While rushing souse
Into a coffee-house,
To find it — Slaughter's!

Or fancy this: —
Walking along the street, some stranger Miss,
Her head with no such thought of danger laden,
When suddenly 'tis "Aries Taurus Virgo!" —
You don't know Latin, I translate it ergo,
Into your Areas a Bull throws the Maiden!

Think of some poor old crone
Treated, just like a penny, with a toss !
At that vile spot now grown
So generally known
For making a Cow Cross !

Nay, fancy your own selves far off from stall,
Or shed, or shop — and that an Ox infuriate
Just pins you to the wall,
Giving you a strong dose of *Oxy-Muriate !*

Methinks I hear the neighbours that live round
The Market-ground
Thus make appeal unto their civic fellows —
" 'Tis well for you that live apart — unable
To hear this brutal Babel,
But our *firesides* are troubled with their *bellows.*"

" Folks that too freely sup
Must e'en put up
With their own troubles if they can't digest ;
But we must needs regard
The case as hard
That *others'* victuals should disturb our rest,
That from our sleep *your* food should start and jump us !
We like, ourselves, a steak,
But, Sirs, for pity's sake !
We don't want oxen at our doors to *rump-us !*

If we *do* doze — it really is too bad!
We constantly are roared awake or rung,
Through bullocks mad
That run in all the 'Night Thoughts' of our
Young!"

Such are the woes of sleepers — now let's take
The woes of those that wish to keep *a Wake!*
Oh think! when Wombwell gives his annual
feasts,
Think of these "Bulls of Basan," far from mild
ones;
Such fierce tame beasts,
That nobody much cares to see the Wild ones!

Think of the Show woman, "what shows a
Dwarf,"
Seeing a red Cow come
To swallow her Tom Thumb,
And forced with broom of birch to keep her off!

Think, too, of Messrs. Richardson and Co.,
When looking at their public private boxes,
To see in the back row
Three live sheep's heads, a porker's and an Ox's!
Think of their Orchestra, when two horns come
Through, to accompany the double drum!

Or, in the midst of murder and remorses,
Just when the Ghost is certain,

A great rent in the curtain,
And enter two tall skeletons — of Horses!

Great Philanthropics! pray urge these topics!
Upon the Solemn Councils of the Nation,
Get a Bill soon, and give, some noon,
The Bulls, a Bull of Excommunication!

Let the old Fair have fair-play as its right,
And to each show and sight
Ye shall be treated with a Free List latitude;
To Richardson's Stage Dramas,
Dio — and Cosmo — ramas,
Giants and Indians wild,
Dwarf, Sea Bear, and Fat Child,
And that most rare of Shows — a Show of Gratitude!

ODE FOR ST. CECILIA'S EVE.

"Look out for squalls." — The Pilot.

O come, dear Barney Isaacs, come,
Punch for one night can spare his drum
As well as pipes of Pan!
Forget not, Popkins, your bassoon,
Nor, Mister Bray, your horn, as soon
As you can leave the Van;

Blind Billy, bring your violin;
Miss Crow you 're great in Cherry Ripe!
And Chubb, your viol must drop in
Its bass to Soger Tommy's pipe.
Ye butchers, bring your bones:
An organ would not be amiss;
If grinding Jim has spouted his,
Lend your's, good Mister Jones.
Do, hurdy-gurdy Jenny,— do
Keep sober for an hour or two,
Music 's charms to help to paint.
And, Sandy Gray, if you should not
Your bagpipes bring — O tuneful Scot!
Conceive the feelings of the Saint!

Miss Strummel issues an invite,
For music, and turn-out to night
In honour of Cecilia's session;
But ere you go, one moment stop,
And with all kindness let me drop
A hint to you, and your profession;
Imprimis then: Pray keep within
The bounds to which your skill was born;
Let the one-handed let alone
Trombone,
Don't — Rheumatiz! seize the violin,
Or Ashmy snatch the horn!
Don't ever to such rows give birth,
As if you had no end on earth,
Except to "wake the lyre;"

Don't "strike the harp," pray never do,
Till others long to strike it too,
Perpetual harping 's apt to tire;
Oh I have heard such flat-and-sharpers,
 I 've blest the head
 Of good King Ned,
For scragging all those old Welsh Harpers!

Pray, never, ere each tuneful doing,
Take a prodigious deal of wooing;
And then sit down to thrum the strain,
As if you 'd never rise again —
The least Cecilia-like of things;
Remember that the Saint has wings.
I 've known Miss Strummel pause an hour,
Ere she could "Pluck the Fairest Flower."
Yet without hesitation, she
Plunged next into the "Deep, Deep Sea,"
And when on the keys she *does* begin,
Such awful torments soon you share,
She really seems like Milton's "Sin,"
 Holding the keys of — you know where!

Never tweak people's ears so toughly,
That urchin-like they can't help saying —
"O dear! O dear — you call this playing,
But oh, it 's playing very roughly!"
Oft, in the ecstasy of pain,
I 've cursed all instrumental workmen,
Wished Broadwood Thurtelled in a lane,

And Kirke White's fate to every Kirkman —
I really once delighted spied
"Clementi Collard" in Cheapside.

Another word, — don't be surprised,
Revered and ragged street Musicians,
You have been only half-baptized,
And each name proper, or improper,
Is not the value of a copper,
Till it has had the due additions,
Husky, Rusky,
Ninny, Tinny,
Hummel, Bummel,
Bowski, Wowski,
All these are very good selectables;
But none of your plain pudding-and-tames —
Folks that are called the hardest names
Are music's most respectables.
Ev'ry woman, ev'ry man,
Look as foreign as you can,
Don't cut your hair, or wash your skin,
Make ugly faces and begin.

Each Dingy Orpheus gravely hears.
And now to show they understand it!
Miss Crow her scrannel throttle clears,
And all the rest prepare to band it.
Each scraper ripe for concertante,
Rozins the hair of Rozinante:
Then all sound A, if they know which,

That they may join like birds in June:
Jack Tar alone neglects to tune,
For he 's all over concert-pitch.

A little prelude goes before,
Like a knock and ring at music's door,
Each instrument gives in its name;
Then sitting in
They all begin
To play a musical round game.
Scrapenberg, as the eldest hand,
Leads a first fiddle to the band,
A second follows suit;
Anon the ace of Horns comes plump
On the two fiddles with a trump,
Puffindorf plays a flute.
This sort of musical revoke,
The grave bassoon begins to smoke
And in rather grumpy kind
Of tone begins to speak its mind;
The double drum is next to mix,
Playing the Devil on Two Sticks —
Clamour, clamour,
Hammer, hammer,
While now and then a pipe is heard,
Insisting to put in a word,
With all his shrilly best,
So to allow the little minion
Time to deliver his opinion,
They take a few bars rest.

Well, little Pipe begins — with sole
And small voice going thro' the *hole*,
Beseeching,
Preaching,
Squealing,
Appealing,
Now as high as he can go,
Now in language rather low,
And having done — begins once more,
Verbatim what he said before.
This twiddling twaddling sets on fire
All the old instrumental ire,
And fiddles for explosion ripe,
Put out the little squeaker's pipe ;
This wakes bass viol — and viol for that,
Seizing on innocent little B flat,
Shakes it like terrier shaking a rat —
They all seem miching malico !
To judge from a rumble unawares,
The drum has had a pitch down stairs ;
And the trumpet rash,
By a violent crash,
Seems splitting somebody's calico !
The viol too groans in deep distress,
As if he suddenly grew sick ;
And one rapid fiddle sets off express,—
Hurrying,
Scurrying,
Spattering,
Clattering,

To fetch him a Doctor of Music.
This tumult sets the Haut-boy crying
Beyond the Piano's pacifying,
The cymbal
Gets nimble,
Triangle
Must wrangle,
The band is becoming most martial of bands,
When just in the middle,
A quakerly fiddle,
Proposes a general shaking of hands!
Quaking,
Shaking,
Quivering,
Shivering,
Long bow — short bow — each bow drawing:
Some like filing,— some like sawing;
At last these agitations cease,
And they all get
The flageolet,
To breathe "a piping time of peace."
Ah, too deceitful charm,
Like light'ning before death,
For Scrapenberg to rest his arm,
And Puffindorf get breath!
Again without remorse or pity,
They play "The Storming of a City,"
Miss S. herself composed and planned it —
When lo! at this renewed attack,
Up jumps a little man in black,—

"The very Devil cannot stand it!"
And with that,
Snatching hat,
(Not his own,)
Off is flown,
Thro' the door,
In his black,
To come back,
Never, never, never more!

Oh Music! praises thou hast had,
From Dryden and from Pope,
For thy good notes, yet none I hope,
But I, e'er praised the bad,
Yet are not saint and sinner even?
Miss Strummel on Cecilia's level?
One drew an angel down from heaven!
The other scared away the Devil! —

A BLOW-UP.

"Here we go up, up, up." — THE LAY OF THE FIRST MINSTREL.

NEAR Battle, Mr. Peter Baker
Was Powder-maker,
Not Alderman Flower's flour, — the white that puffs

And primes and loads heads bald, or gray, or
chowder,
Figgins and Higgins, Fippins, Filby, Crowder,—
Not vile apothecary's pounded stuffs,
But something blacker, bloodier, and louder,
Gun-powder!

This stuff, as people know, is *semper*
Eadem; very hasty in its temper—
Like Honour that resents the gentlest taps
Mere semblances of blows, however slight;
So powder fires, although you only p'rhaps
Strike light.
To make it, therefore, is a ticklish business,
And sometimes gives both head and heart a dizzi-
ness,
For as all human flash and fancy minders,
Frequenting fights and Powder-works well know,
There seldom is a mill without a blow
Sometimes upon the grinders.
But then—the melancholy phrase to soften,
Mr. B.'s mill *transpired* so very often!
And advertised—than all Price Currents
louder,
"Fragments look up—there is a rise in Pow-
der,"
So frequently, it caused the neighbours' won-
der,—
And certain people had the inhumanity
To lay it all to Mr. Baker's vanity,

That he might have to say — "That was *my*
thunder!"
One day — so goes the tale,
Whether, with iron hoof,
Not sparkle-proof,
Some ninny-hammer struck upon a nail, —
Whether some glow-worm of the Guy Faux
stamp,
Crept in the building, with Unsafety Lamp —
One day this mill that had by water ground,
Became a sort of windmill and blew round.
With bounce that went in sound as far as Dover, it
Sent half the workmen sprawling to the sky;
Besides some visitors who gained thereby,
What they had asked — permission "to go over it!"
Of course it was a very hard and high blow,
And somewhat differed from what 's called a
flyblow
At Cowes' Regatta as I once observed,
A pistol-shot made twenty vessels start;
If such a sound could terrify oak's heart,
Think how this crash the human nerve unnerved.
In fact, it was a very awful thing, —
As people know that have been used to battle,
In springing either mine or mill, you spring
A precious rattle!
The dunniest heard it — poor old Mr. F.
Doubted for once if he was ever deaf;
Through Tunbridge town it caused most strange
alarms,

Mr. and Mrs. Fogg,
Who lived like cat and dog,
Were shocked for once into each other's arms.
Miss M. the milliner — her fright so strong,
Made a great gobble-stitch six inches long;
The veriest quakers quaked against their wish:
The "Best of Sons" was taken unawares,
And kicked the "Best of Parents" down the stairs:
The steadiest servant dropped the China dish;
A thousand started, though there was but one
Fated to win, and that was Mister Dunn,
Who struck convulsively, and hooked a fish!

Miss Wiggins, with some grass upon her fork,
Tossed it just like a haymaker at work;
Her sister not in any better case,
For, taking wine,
With nervous Mr. Pyne,
He jerked his glass of Sherry in her face.
Poor Mistress Davy,
Bobbed off her bran-new turban in the gravy;
While Mr. Davy at the lower end,
Preparing for a Goose a carver's labour,
Darted his two-pronged weapon in his neighbour,
As if for once he meant to help a friend.

The nurse-maid telling little "Jack-a-Norey,"
"Bo-peep" and "Blue-cap" at the house's top,
Screamed, and let Master Jeremiah drop

From a fourth story!
Nor yet did matters any better go
With Cook and Housemaid in the realms below;
As for the Laundress, timid Martha Gunning,
Expressing faintness and her fear by fits
And starts, — she came at last but to her wits,
By falling in the ale that John left running.

Grave Mr. Miles, the meekest of mankind,
Struck all at once, deaf, stupid, dumb, and blind,
Sat in his chaise some moments like a corse,
Then coming to his mind,
Was shocked to find,
Only a pair of shafts without a horse.
Out scrambled all the Misses from Miss Joy's!
From Prospect House, for urchins small and big,
Hearing the awful noise,
Out rushed a flood of boys,
Floating a man in black, without a wig; —
Some carried out one treasure, some another,—
Some caught their tops and taws up in a hurry,
Some saved Chambaud, some rescued Lindley Murray, —
But little Tiddy carried his big brother!
Sick of such terrors,
The Tunbridge folks resolved that truth should dwell
No longer secret in a Tunbridge Well,
But to warn Baker of his dangerous errors;
Accordingly to bring the point to pass,

They called a meeting of the broken glass,
The shattered chimney pots, and scattered tiles,
The damage of each part,
And packed it in a cart,
Drawn by the horse that ran from Mr. Miles;
While Doctor Babblethorpe, the worthy Rector,
And Mr. Gammage, cutler to George Rex,
And some few more, whose names would only vex,
Went as a deputation to the Ex
Powder-proprietor and Mill-director.

Now Mr. Baker's dwelling-house had pleased
Along with mill-materials to roam,
And for a time the deputies were teased,
To find the noisy gentleman at home;
At last they found him with undamaged skin,
Safe at the Tunbridge Arms — not out — but Inn.

The worthy Rector, with uncommon zeal,
Soon put his spoke in for the common weal —
A grave old gentlemanly kind of Urban,—
The piteous tale of Jeremiah moulded,
And then unfolded,
By way of climax, Mrs. Davy's turban;
He told how auctioneering Mr. Pidding
Knocked down a lot without a bidding,—
How Mr. Miles, in fright, had given his mare,
The whip she wouldn't bear,—
At Prospect House, how Doctor Oates, not Titus,

Danced like Saint Vitus, —
And Mr. Beak, thro' Powder's misbehaving,
Cut off his nose whilst shaving ; —
When suddenly, with words that seemed like swearing,
Beyond a Licenser's belief or bearing —
Broke in the stuttering, sputtering Mr. Gammage —
Who is to pay us, Sir — he argued thus,
" For loss of cus-cus-cus-cus-cus-cus-cus —
Cus-custom, and the dam-dam-dam-dam-damage ?

Now many a person had been fairly puzzled
By such assailants, and completely muzzled ;
Baker, however, was not dashed with ease —
But proved he practised after their own system,
And with small ceremony soon dismissed 'em,
Putting these words into their ears like fleas ;
" If I do have a blow, well, where 's the oddity ?
I merely do as other tradesmen do,
You, Sir, — and you — and you !
I 'm only puffing off my own commodity ! "

THE GHOST.

A VERY SERIOUS BALLAD.

"I'll be your second." — LISTON.

IN Middle Row, some years ago,
  There lived one Mr. Brown;
And many folks considered him
  The stoutest man in town.

But Brown and stout will both wear out,
  One Friday he died hard,
And left a widowed wife to mourn
  At twenty pence a yard.

Now widow B. in two short months
  Thought mourning quite a tax;
And wished, like Mr. Wilberforce,
  To *manumit* her blacks.

With Mr. Street she soon was sweet;
  The thing thus came about:
She asked him in at home, and then
  At church he asked her out!

Assurance such as this the man
  In ashes could not stand;
So like a Phœnix he rose up
  Against the Hand in Hand.

One dreary night the angry sprite
  Appeared before her view;
It came a little after one,
  But she was after two!

"Oh Mrs. B., oh Mrs. B.!
  Are these your sorrow's deeds,
Already getting up a flame,
  To burn your widow's weeds?

"It 's not so long since I have left
  For aye the mortal scene;
My Memory — like Rogers's,
  Should still be bound in green!

"Yet if my face you still retrace
  I almost have a doubt —
I 'm like an old Forget-Me-Not,
  With all the leaves torn out!

"To think that on that finger joint,
  Another pledge should cling;
Oh Bess! upon my very soul,
  It struck like 'Knock and Ring.'

"A ton of marble on my breast
Can't hinder my return;
Your conduct, Ma'am, has set my blood
A-boiling in my urn!

"Remember, oh! remember, how
The marriage 'rite did run, —
If ever we one flesh should be,
'Tis now — when I have none!

"And you, Sir — once a bosom friend —
Of perjured faith convict,
As ghostly toe can give no blow,
Consider you are kicked.

"A hollow voice is all I have,
But this I tell you plain,
Marry come up! — you marry Ma'am,
And I'll come up again."

More he had said, but chanticleer
The spritely shade did shock
With sudden crow, and off he went,
Like fowling-piece at cock!

ODE TO MADAME HENGLER,

FIREWORK-MAKER TO VAUXHALL.

Oh, Mrs. Hengler! — Madame, — I beg pardon
Starry Enchantress of the Surrey Garden!
Accept an Ode not meant as any scoff —
The Bard were bold indeed at thee to quiz,
Whose squibs are far more popular than his;
Whose works are much more certain to go off.

Great is thy fame, but not a silent fame;
With many a bang the public ear it courts;
And yet thy arrogance we never blame,
But take thy merits from thy own reports.
Thou hast indeed the most indulgent backers,
We make no doubting, misbelieving comments,
Even in thy most bounceable of moments;
But lend our ears implicit to thy crackers! —
Strange helps to thy applause too are not missing,
Thy Rockets raise thee,
And Serpents praise thee,
As none beside are ever praised — by hissing!

Mistress of Hydropyrics,
Of glittering Pindarics, Sapphics, Lyrics,

Professor of a Fiery Necromancy,
Oddly thou charmest the politer sorts
With midnight sports,
Partaking very much of *flash* and *fancy!*

What thoughts had shaken all
In olden time at thy nocturnal revels, —
Each brimstone ball,
They would have deemed an eyeball of the Devil's!
But now thy flaming Meteors cause no fright;
A modern Hubert to the royal ear,
Might whisper without fear,
"My Lord, they say there were five moons to night!"
Nor would it raise one superstitious notion
To hear the whole description fairly out: —
"One fixed — which t'other four whirled round about
With wond'rous motion."

Such are the very sights
Thou workest, Queen of Fire, on earth and heaven,
Between the hours of midnight and eleven,
Turning our English to Arabian Nights,
With blazing mounts, and founts, and scorching dragons,
Blue stars and white,
And blood-red light,

And dazzling Wheels fit for Enchanters' wagons.
Thrice lucky woman! doing things that be
With other folks past benefit of parson;
For burning, no Burn's Justice falls on thee,
Altho' night after night the public see
Thy Vauxhall palaces all end in Arson!

Sure thou wast never born
Like old Sir Hugh, with water in thy head,
Nor lectured night and morn
Of sparks and flames to have an awful dread,
Allowed by a prophetic dam and sire
To play with fire.
O didst thou never, in those days gone by,
Go carrying about — no schoolboy prouder —
Instead of waxen doll a little Guy;
Or in thy pretty pyrotechnic vein,
Up the parental pigtail lay a train,
To let off all his powder?

Full of the wildfire of thy youth,
Did'st never in plain truth,
Plant whizzing Flowers in thy mother's pots,
Turning the garden into powder plots?
Or give the cook, to fright her,
Thy paper sausages well stuffed with nitre?
Nay, wert thou never guilty, now, of dropping
A lighted cracker by thy sister's Dear,
So that she could not hear
The question he was popping?

Go on, Madame! Go on — be bright and busy
While hoaxed Astronomers look up and stare
From tall observatories, dumb and dizzy,
So see a Squib in Cassiopeia's Chair!
A Serpent wriggling into Charles's Wain!
A Roman Candle lighting the Great Bear!
A Rocket tangled in Diana's train,
And Crackers stuck in Berenice's Hair!

There is a King of Fire — Thou shouldst be
    Queen!
Methinks a good connection might come from it;
Could'st thou not make him, in the garden scene,
Set out per Rocket and return per Comet;
        Then give him a hot treat
Of Pyrotechnicals to sit and sup,
Lord! how the world would throng to see him eat,
He swallowing fire, while thou dost throw it up!

One solitary night — true is the story,
Watching those forms that Fancy will create
Within the bright confusion of the grate,
I saw a dazzling countenance of glory!
        Oh Dei gratias!
        That fiery facias
'Twas thine, Enchantress of the Surrey Grove;
        And ever since that night,
        In dark and bright,
Thy face is *registered* within my *stove!*

Long may that starry brow enjoy its rays,
May no untimely *blow* its doom forestall;
But when old age prepares the friendly pall,
When the last spark of all thy sparks decays,
Then die lamented by good people all,
Like Goldsmith's *Madam Blaize!*

THE DOUBLE KNOCK.

RAT-TAT it went upon the lion's chin,
"That hat, I know it!" cried the joyful girl;
"Summer's it is, I know him by his knock,
Comers like him are welcome as the day!
Lizzy! go down and open the street-door,
Busy I am to any one but *him.*
Know him you must — he has been often here;
Show him up stairs, and tell him I'm alone."

Quickly the maid went tripping down the stair;
Thickly the heart of Rose Matilda beat;
"Sure he has brought me tickets for the play —
Drury — or Covent Garden — darling man! —
Kemble will play — or Kean who makes the soul
Tremble; in Richard or the frenzied Moor —
Farren, the stay and prop of many a farce
Barren beside — or Liston, Laughter's Child —
Kelly the natural, to witness whom
Jelly is nothing to the public's jam —

Cooper, the sensible — and Walter Knowles
Super, in William Tell — now rightly told.
Better — perchance, from Andrews, brings a box,
Letter of boxes for the Italian stage —
Brocard! Donzelli! Taglioni! Paul!
No card,— thank heaven — engages me to night!
Feathers, of course, no turban, and no toque —
Weather 's against it, but I 'll go in curls.
Dearly I dote on white — my satin dress,
Merely one night — it won't be much the worse —
Cupid — the New Ballet I long to see —
Stupid! why don't she go and ope the door!"

Glistened her eye as the impatient girl
Listened, low bending o'er the topmost stair.
Vainly, alas! she listens and she bends,
Plainly she hears this question and reply:
"Axes your pardon, Sir, but what d'ye want?"
"Taxes," says he, "and shall not call again!"

LINES TO MARY.

(AT NO. 1, NEWGATE, FAVOURED BY MR. WONTNER.)

O Mary, I believed you true,
And I was blest in so believing;
But till this hour I never knew —
That you were taken up for thieving!

Oh! when I snatched a tender kiss,
Or some such trifle when I courted,
You said, indeed, that love was bliss,
But never owned you were transported!

But then to gaze on that fair face —
It would have been an unfair feeling,
To dream that you had pilfered lace —
And Flints had suffered from your stealing!

Or when my suit I first preferred,
To bring your coldness to repentance,
Before I hammered out a word,
How could I dream you'd heard a sentence!

Or when with all the warmth of youth
I strove to prove my love no fiction,
How could I guess I urged a truth
On one already past conviction!

How could I dream that ivory part,
Your hand — where I have looked and lingered,
Altho' it stole away my heart,
Had been held up as one light-fingered!

In melting verse your charms I drew,
The charms in which my muse delighted —
Alas! the lay, I thought was new,
Spoke only what had been *indicted!*

Oh! when that form, a lovely one,
Hung on the neck its arms had flown to,
I little thought that you had run
A chance of hanging on your own too.

You said you picked me from the world,
My vanity it now must shock it —
And down at once my pride is hurled,
You 've picked me — and you 've picked a pocket!

Oh! when our love had got so far,
The banns were read by Dr. Daly,
Who asked if there was any *bar* —
Why did not some one shout "Old Bailey?"

But when you robed your flesh and bones
In that pure white that angel garb is,
Who could have thought you, Mary Jones,
Among the Joans that link with *Darbies*?

And when the parson came to say,
My goods were yours, if I had got any,
And you should honour and obey,
Who could have thought — "O Bay of Botany."

But, oh, — the worst of all your slips
I did not till this day discover —
That down in Deptford's prison ships,
Oh, Mary! you 've a hulking lover!

NO. II.

"Love, with a witness!"

He has shaved off his whiskers and blackened
his brows,
Wears a patch and a wig of false hair,—
But it 's him — Oh it 's him! — we exchanged
lovers' vows,
When I lived up in Cavendish Square.

He had beautiful eyes, and his lips were the same,
And his voice was as soft as a flute —
Like a Lord or a Marquis he looked, when he
came,
To make love in his master's best suit.

If I lived for a thousand long years from my
birth,
I shall never forget what he told;
How he loved me beyond the rich women of earth,
With their jewels and silver and gold!

When he kissed me and bade me adieu with a
sigh,
By the light of the sweetest of moons,
Oh how little I dreamt I was bidding good-bye
To my Missis's teapot and spoons!

NO. III.

"I'd be a Parody." — BAILEY.

WE met — t'was in a mob — and I thought he
had done me —
I felt — I could not feel — for no watch was upon
me;
He ran — the night was cold — and his pace was
unaltered,
I too longed much to pelt — but my small-boned
legs faltered.
I wore my bran new boots — and unrivalled their
brightness,
They fit me to a hair — how I hated their tight-
ness!
I called, but no one came, and my stride had a
tether
Oh *thou* hast been the cause of this anguish, my
leather!

And once again we met — and an old pal was
near him,
He swore, a something low — but 'twas no use to
fear him;
I seized upon his arm, he was mine and mine
only,
And stept — as he deserved — to cells wretched
and lonely:
And there he will be tried — but I shall ne'er
receive her,

The watch that went too sure for an artful de-
    ceiver;
The world may think me gay, — heart and feet
    ache together,
Oh *thou* hast been the cause of this anguish, my
    leather.

FRENCH AND ENGLISH.

"Good heaven! Why even the little children in France speak French!" ADDISON.

I.

NEVER go to France
Unless you know the lingo,
  If you do, like me,
You will repent by jingo.
Staring like a fool,
And silent as a mummy,
There I stood alone,
A nation with a dummy:

II.

Chaises stand for chairs,
They christen letters *Billies*,
They call their mothers *mares*,
And all their daughters *fillies*;

Strange it was to hear,
I 'll tell you what 's a good 'un,
They call their leather *queer*,
And half their shoes are wooden.

III.

Signs I had to make,
For every little notion,
Limbs all going like
A telegraph in motion,
For wine I reeled about,
To show my meaning fully,
And made a pair of horns,
To ask for "beef and bully."

IV.

Moo! I cried for milk;
I got my sweet things snugger,
When I kissed Jeannette,
'Twas understood for sugar.
If I wanted bread,
My jaws I set a-going,
And asked for new-laid eggs.
By clapping hands and crowing!

V.

If I wished a ride,
I 'll tell you how I got it;
On my stick astride,
I made believe to trot it;

Then their cash was strange,
It bored me every minute,
Now here's a *hog* to change,
How many *sows* are in it!

VI.

Never go to France,
Unless you know the lingo;
If you do, like me,
You will repent, by jingo;
Staring like a fool,
And silent as a mummy,
There I stood alone,
A nation with a dummy!

OUR VILLAGE.—BY A VILLAGER.

Our village, that's to say, not Miss Mitford's village, but our village of Bullock Smithy,
Is come into by an avenue of trees, three oak pollards, two elders, and a withy;
And in the middle, there's a green of about not exceeding an acre and a half;
It's common to all, and fed off by nineteen cows, six ponies, three horses, five asses, two foals, seven pigs, and a calf!

Besides a pond in the middle, as is held by a similar sort of common law lease,
And contains twenty ducks, six drakes, three ganders, two dead dogs, four drowned kittens' and twelve geese.
Of course the green 's cropt very close, and does famous for bowling when the little village boys play at cricket;
Only some horse, or pig, or cow, or great jackass, is sure to come and stand right before the wicket.
There 's fifty-five private houses, let alone barns and workshops, and pigstyes, and poultry huts, and such-like sheds;
With plenty of public-houses — two Foxes, one Green Man, three Bunch of Grapes, one Crown, and six King's Heads.
The Green Man is reckoned the best, as the only one that for love or money can raise
A postilion, a blue jacket, two deplorable lame white horses, and a ramshackled "neat post-chaise."
There 's one parish church for all the people, whatsoever may be their ranks in life or their degrees,
Except one very damp, small, dark, freezing-cold, little Methodist chapel of Ease;
And close by the churchyard, there 's a stonemason's yard, that when the time is seasonable

Will furnish with afflictions sore and marble urns
and cherubims very low and reasonable.
There 's a cage, comfortable enough ; I 've been
in it with Old Jack Jeffrey and Tom Pike ;
For the Green Man next door will send you in
ale, gin, or any thing else you like.
I can't speak of the stocks, as nothing remains of
them but the upright post ;
But the pound is kept in repairs for the sake of
Cob's horse, as is always there almost.
There 's a smithy of course, where that queer
sort of a chap in his way, Old Joe Bradley,
Perpetually hammers and stammers, for he stut-
ters and shoes horses very badly.
There 's a shop of all sorts, that sells every thing,
kept by the widow of Mr. Task ;
But when you go there it 's ten to one she 's out
of every thing you ask.
You 'll know her house by the swarm of boys,
like flies, about the old sugary cask :
There are six empty houses, and not so well
papered inside as out,
For billstickers won't beware, but stick notices of
sales and election placards all about.
That 's the Doctor's with a green door, where the
garden pots in the windows is seen ;
A weakly monthly rose that don't blow, and a
dead geranium, and a tea-plant with five
black leaves and one green.

As for hollyoaks at the cottage doors, and honeysuckles and jasmines, you may go and whistle;
But the Tailor's front garden grows two cabbages, a dock, a ha'porth of pennyroyal, two dandelions, and a thistle.
There are three small orchards — Mr. Busby's the schoolmaster's is the chief —
With two pear-trees that don't bear; one plum and an apple, that every year is stripped by a thief.
There's another small day-school too, kept by the respectable Mrs. Gaby.
A select establishment, for six little boys and one big, and four little girls and a baby;
There's a rectory, with pointed gables and strange odd chimneys that never smokes,
For the rector don't live on his living like other Christian sort of folks;
There's a barber's, once a-week well filled with rough black-bearded shock-headed churls,
And a window with two feminine men's heads, and two masculine ladies in false curls;
There's a butcher's, and a carpenter's, and a plumber's, and a small green-grocer's, and a baker,
But he won't bake on a Sunday, and there's a sexton that's a coal merchant besides, and an undertaker;
And a toy-shop, but not a whole one, for a village can't compare with the London shops;

One window sells drums, dolls, kites, carts, batts,
Clout's balls, and the other sells malt and hops.
And Mrs. Brown, in domestic economy not to be a bit behind her betters,
Lets her house to a milliner, a watchmaker, a rat-catcher, a cobbler, lives in it herself, and it 's the post-office for letters.
Now I 've gone through all the village — ay, from end to end, save and except one more house,
But I haven't come to that — and I hope I never shall — and that 's the Village Poor-House!

A TRUE STORY.

Whoe'er has seen upon the human face
The yellow jaundice and the jaundice black,
May form a notion of old Colonel Case
With nigger Pompey waiting at his back.

Case, — as the case is, many time with folks
From hot Bengal, Calcutta, or Bombay,
Had tint his tint, as Scottish tongues would say,
And showed two cheeks as yellow as eggs' yolks.
Pompey, the chip of some old ebon block,
In hue was like his master's stiff cravat,

And might indeed have claimed akin to *that*,
Coming, as *he* did, of an old *black stock*.

Case wore the liver's livery that such
Must wear, their past excesses to denote,
Like Greenwich pensioners that take too much,
And then do penance in a yellow coat.
Pompey's, a deep and permanent jet dye,
A stain of nature's staining — one of those
We call *fast* colours — merely, I suppose,
Because such colours never *go* or *fly*.

Pray mark this difference of dark and sallow,
Pompey's black husk, and the old Colonel's yellow.

The Colonel, once a pennyless beginner,
From a long Indian rubber rose a winner,
With plenty of pagodas in his pocket,
And homeward turning his Hibernian thought,
Deemed *Wicklow* was the very place that ought
To harbour one whose *wick* was in the socket.

Unhappily for Case's scheme of quiet,
Wicklow just then was in a pretty riot,
A fact recorded in each day's diurnals,
Things, Case was not accustomed to peruse,
Careless of news;
But Pompey always read these bloody journals,
Full of Killmany and of Killmore work,
The freaks of some O'Shaunessy's shillaly,

Of morning frays by some O'Brien Burke,
Or horrid nightly outrage by some Daly;
How scums deserving of the Devil's ladle,
Would fall upon the harmless scull and knock it,
And if he found an infant in the cradle
Stern Rock would hardly hesitate to rock it; —
In fact, he read of burner and of killer,
And Irish ravages, day after day,
Till, haunting in his dreams, he used to say,
That "Pompey could not sleep on *Pompey's Pillar.*"

Judge then the horror of the nigger's face
To find — with such impressions of that dire land —
That Case, — his master, — was a packing case
For Ireland!
He saw in fearful reveries arise,
Phantasmagorias of those dreadful men
Whose fame associate with Irish plots is,
Fitzgeralds — Tones — O'Connors — Hares — and then
"Those *Emmets*," not so "little in his eyes"
As Doctor Watts's!
He felt himself piked, roasted, — carved and hacked,
His big black burly body seemed in fact
A pincushion for Terror's pins and needles, —
Oh, how he wished himself beneath the sun
Of Afric — or in far Barbadoes — one
Of Bishop Coleridge's new *black beadles.*

Full of this fright,
With broken peace and broken English choking,
As black as any raven and as croaking,
Pompey rushed in upon his master's sight,
Plumped on his knees, and clasped his sable digits,
Thus stirring Curiosity's sharp fidgets —
"O Massa ! — Massa ! — Colonel ! — Massa Case. —
Not go to Ireland ! — Ireland dam bad place ;
Dem take our bloods — dem Irish — every drop —
Oh why for Massa go so far a distance
To have him life ?" —— Here Pompey made a stop,
Putting an awful period to existence.

"Not go to Ireland — not to Ireland, fellow,
And murdered — why should I be murdered, Sirrah ?"
Cried Case, with anger's tinge upon his yellow,—
Pompey, for answer, pointing in a mirror
The Colonel's saffron, and his own japan,—
"Well, what has that to do — quick — speak outright, boy ?
"O Massa" — (so the explanation ran)
"Massa be killed — 'cause Massa *Orange Man*,
And Pompey killed — 'cause Pompey not a *White Boy !*"

THE CARELESSE NURSE MAYD.

I SAWE a Mayd sitte on a Bank,
Beguiled by Wooer fayne and fond;
And whiles His flatterynge Vowes She drank,
Her Nurselynge slipt within a Pond!

All Even Tide they Talkde and Kist,
For She was fayre and He was Kinde;
The Sunne went down before She wist
Another Sonne had sett behinde!

With angrie Hands and frownynge Browe,
That deemd Her owne the Urchine's Sinne,
She pluckt Him out, but he was nowe
Past being Whipt for fallynge in.

She then beginnes to wayle the Ladde
With Shrikes that Echo answered round —
O! foolishe Mayd to be soe sadde
The Momente that her Care was drownd!

TO FANNY.

"Gay being, born to flutter!" — SALE'S GLEE.

Is this your faith, then, Fanny!
  What, to chat with every Dun!
I'm the one, then, but of many,
  Not of many, but the *One!*

Last night you smiled on all, Ma'am,
  That appeared in scarlet dress;
And your Regimental Ball, Ma'am,
  Looked a little like a *Mess*.

I thought that of the Sogers
  (As the Scotch say) one might do,
And that I, slight Ensign Rogers,
  Was the chosen man and true.

But 'Sblood! your eye was busy
  With that ragamuffin mob; —
Colonel Buddell — Colonel Dizzy —
  And Lieutenant-Colonel Cobb.

General Joblin, General Jodkin,
  Colonels — Kelly, Felly, with
Majors — Sturgeon, Truffle, Bodkin,
  And the Quarter-master Smith.

Major Powderum — Major Dowdrum —
  Major Chowdrum — Major Bye —
Captain Tawney — Captain Fawney,
  Captain Any-one — but I!

Deuce take it! when the regiment
  You so praised, I only thought
That you loved it in abridgment,
  But I now am better taught!

I went, as loving man goes,
  To admire thee in quadrilles;
But Fan, you dance fandangoes
  With just any fop that wills!

I went with notes before us,
  On the lay of Love to touch;
But with all the Corps in chorus,
  Oh! it is indeed too much!

You once — ere you contracted
  For the Army — seemed my own;
But now you laugh with all the Staff,
  And I may sigh alone! —

I know not how it chances,
  When my passion ever dares,
But the warmer my advances,
  Then the cooler are your airs.

I am, I don't conceal it,
  But I am a little hurt;
You 're a Fan, and I must feel it,
  Fit for nothing but a *Flirt!*

I dreamt thy smiles of beauty
  On myself alone did fall;
But alas! "Cosi Fan Tutti!"
  It is thus, Fan, thus will all!

You have taken quite a mob in
  Of new military flames;—
They would make a fine Round Robin
  If I gave you all their names!

STANZAS.

WRITTEN UNDER THE FEAR OF BAILIFFS.

Alas! of all the noxious things
  That wait upon the poor,

Most cruel is that Felon-Fear
  That haunts the "Debtor's Door!"

Saint Sepulchre's begins to toll,
  The Sheriffs seek the cell:—
So I expect their officers,
  And tremble at the bell!

I look for *beer*, and yet I quake
  With fright at every *tap*;
And dread a *double-knock*, for oh!
  I 've not a *single rap!*

FUGITIVE LINES ON PAWNING MY WATCH.

"Aurum *pot-a-bile:*"—Gold biles the pot.—FREE TRANSLATION.

FAREWELL then, my golden repeater,
  We 're come to my Uncle's old shop;
And hunger won't be a dumb-waiter,
  The Cerberus growls for a sop!

To quit thee, my comrade diurnal,
  My feelings will certainly scotch;
But oh! there 's a riot internal,
  And Famine calls out for the Watch!

Oh! hunger 's a terrible trial,
  I really must have a relief,—
So here goes the plate of your dial
  To fetch me some Williams's beef!

As famished as any lost seaman,
  I 've fasted for many a dawn,
And now must play chess with the Demon,
  And give it a *check* with a *pawn.*

I 've fasted, since dining at Buncle's,
  Two days with true Perceval zeal —
And now must make up at my Uncle's,
  By getting a *duplicate* meal.

No Peachum it is, or young Lockit,
  That rifles my fob with a snatch;
Alas! I must pick my own pocket,
  And make gravy-soup of my watch!

So long I have wandered a starver,
  I 'm getting as keen as a hawk;
Time's long hand must take up a carver,
  His short hand lay hold of a fork.

Right heavy and sad the event is,
  But oh! it is Poverty's crime;
I 've been such a Brownrigg's Apprentice,
  I thus must be "out of my Time."

Alas! when in Brook Street the upper
  In comfort I lived between walls,
I 've gone to a dance for my supper; —
  But now I must go to Three Balls!

Folks talk about dressing for dinner,
  But I have for dinner undrest;
Since Christmas, as I am a sinner,
  I 've eaten a suit of my best.

I haven't a rag or a mummock
  To fetch me a chop or a steak;
I wish that the coats of my stomach
  Were such as my Uncle would take!

When dishes were ready with garnish
  My watch used to warn with a chime —
But now my repeater must furnish
  The dinner in lieu of the time!

My craving will have no denials,
  I can't fob it off, if you stay,
So go, — and the old Seven Dials
  Must tell me the time of the day.

Your chimes I shall never more hear 'em,
  To part is a Tic Douloureux!
But Tempus has his edax rerum,
  And I have my Feeding-Time too!

Farewell then, my golden repeater,
We 're come to my Uncle's old shop—
And Hunger won't be a dumb-waiter,
The Cerberus growls for a sop!

THE COMPASS, WITH VARIATIONS.

"The Needles have sometimes been fatal to Mariners."—
PICTURE OF ISLE OF WIGHT.

ONE close of day—'t was in the bay
Of Naples, bay of glory!
While light was hanging crowns of gold
On mountains high and hoary,
A gallant bark got under weigh,
And with her sails my story.

For Leghorn she was bound direct,
With wine and oil for cargo,
Her crew of men some nine or ten,
The captain's name was Iago;
A good and gallant bark she was,
La Donna (called) del Lago.

Bronzed mariners were hers to view,
With brown cheeks, clear or muddy,

Dark, shining eyes, and coal-black hair,
Meet heads for painter's study;
But 'midst their tan there stood one man,
Whose cheek was fair and ruddy;

His brow was high, a loftier brow
Ne'er shone in song or sonnet,
His hair a little scant, and when
He doffed his cap or bonnet,
One saw that Grey had gone beyond
A premiership upon it!

His eye — a passenger was he,
The cabin he had hired it, —
His eye was grey, and when he looked
Around, the prospect fired it —
A fine poetic light, as if
The Appe-Nine inspired it.

His frame was stout, in height about
Six feet — well made and portly;
Of dress and manner just to give
A sketch, but very shortly,
His order seemed a composite
Of rustic with the courtly.

He ate and quaffed, and joked and laughed
And chatted with the seamen,
And often tasked their skill and asked
"What weather is 't to be, man?"

No demonstration there appeared
That he was any demon.

No sort of sign there was that he
Could raise a stormy rumpus,
Like Prospero make breezes blow,
And rocks and billows thump us,—
But little we supposed what he
Could with the needle compass!

Soon came a storm — the sea at first
Seemed lying almost fallow —
When lo! full crash, with billowy dash,
From clouds of black and yellow,
Came such a gale, as blows but once
A century, like the aloe!

Our stomachs we had just prepared
To vest a small amount in;
When, gush! a flood of brine came down
The skylight — quite a fountain,
And right on end the table reared,
Just like the Table Mountain.

Down rushed the soup, down gushed the wine,
Each roll, its rôle repeating,
Rolled down — the round of beef declared
For parting — not for meating!
Off flew the fowls, and all the game
Was "too far gone for eating!"

Down knife and fork — down went the pork,
The lamb too broke its tether;
Down mustard went — each condiment —
Salt — pepper — all together!
Down every thing, like craft that seek
The Downs in stormy weather.

Down plunged the Lady of the Lake,
Her timbers seemed to sever;
Down, down, a dreary derry down,
Such lurch she had gone never;
She almost seemed about to take
A bed of down for ever!

Down dropt the captain's nether jaw,
Thus robbed of all its uses,
He thought he saw the Evil One
Beside Vesuvian sluices,
Playing at dice for soul and ship,
And throwing *Sink* and *Deuces.*

Down fell the steward on his face,
To all the Saints commending;
And candles to the Virgin vowed,
As save-alls 'gainst his ending.
Down fell the mate, he thought his fate,
Check-mate, was close impending!

Down fell the cook — the cabin boy,
Their beads with fervor telling,

While alps of surge, with snowy verge,
Above the yards came yelling.
Down fell the crew, and on their knees
Shuddered at each white swelling!

Down sunk the sun of bloody hue,
His crimson light a cleaver
To each red rover of a wave:
To eye of fancy-weaver,
Neptune, the God, seemed tossing in
A raging scarlet fever!

Sore, sore afraid, each papist prayed
To Saint and Virgin Mary;
But one there was that stood composed
Amid the waves' vagary;
As stanch as rock, a true game cock
'Mid chicks of Mother Carey!

His ruddy cheek retained its streak,
No danger seemed to shrink him:
His step still bold,— of mortal mould
The crew could hardly think him:
The Lady of the Lake, he seemed
To know, could never sink him.

Relaxed at last the furious gale
Quite out of breath with racing;
The boiling flood in milder mood,
With gentler billows chasing;

From stem to stern, with frequent turn,
The Stranger took to pacing.

And as he walked to self he talked,
Some ancient ditty thrumming,
In under tone, as not alone —
Now whistling, and now humming —
"You're welcome, Charlie," "Cowdenknowes,"
"Kenmure," or "Campbells' Coming."

Down went the wind, down went the wave,
Fear quitted the most finical;
The Saints, I wot, were soon forgot,
And Hope was at the pinnacle:
When rose on high, a frightful cry —
"The Devil 's in the binnacle!"

"The Saints be near," the helmsman cried,
His voice with quite a falter —
"Steady 's my helm, but every look
The needle seems to alter;
God only knows where China lies,
Jamaica, or Gibraltar!"

The captain stared aghast at mate,
The pilot at the apprentice;
No fancy of the German Sea
Of Fiction the event is:
But when they at the compass looked,
It seemed non compass mentis.

Now north, now south, now east, now west,
The wavering point was shaken,
'T was past the whole philosophy
Of Newton, or of Bacon;
Never by compass, till that hour,
Such latitudes were taken!

With fearful speech, each after each
Took turns in the inspection;
They found no gun — no iron — none
To vary its direction;
It seemed a new magnetic case
Of Poles in Insurrection!

Farewell to wives, farewell their lives,
And all their household riches;
Oh! while they thought of girl or boy,
And dear domestic niches,
All down the side which holds the heart,
That needle gave them stitches.

With deep amaze, the Stranger gazed
To see them so white-livered:
And walked abaft the binnacle,
To know at what they shivered;
But when he stood beside the card,
St. Josef! how it quivered!

No fancy-motion, brain-begot,
In eye of timid dreamer —

The nervous finger of a sot
Ne'er showed a plainer tremor;
To every brain it seemed too plain,
There stood the Infernal Schemer!

Mixed brown and blue each visage grew,
Just like a pullet's gizzard;
Meanwhile the captain's wandering wit,
From tacking like an izzard,
Bore down in this plain course at last,
"It 's Michael Scott — the Wizard!"

A smile past o'er the ruddy face,
"To see the poles so falter,
I 'm puzzled, friends, as much as you,
For with no fiends I palter;
Michael I 'm not — although a Scott —
My Christian name is Walter."

Like oil it fell, that name, a spell
On all the fearful faction;
The Captain's head (for he had read)
Confessed the Needle's action,
And bowed to HIM in whom the North
Has lodged its main attraction!

PAIRED *NOT* MATCHED.

Of wedded bliss
Bards sing amiss,
I cannot make a song of it;
For I am small,
My wife is tall,
And that 's the short and long of it!

When we debate
It is my fate
To always have the wrong of it;
For I am small
And she is tall,
And that 's the short and long of it;

And when I speak
My voice is weak,
But hers — she makes a gong of it;
For I am small,
And she is tall,
And that 's the short and long of it;

She has, in brief,
Command in Chief,
And I 'm but Aide-de-camp of it;

For I am small,
And she is tall,
And that 's the short and long of it!

She gives to me
The weakest tea,
And takes the whole Souchong of it;
For I am small,
And she is tall,
And that 's the short and long of it;

She 'll sometimes grip
My buggy whip,
And make me feel the thong of it;
For I am small,
And she is tall,
And that 's the short and long of it!

Against my life
She 'll take a knife,
Or fork, and dart the prong of it;
For I am small,
And she is tall,
And that 's the short and long of it!

I sometimes think
I 'll take to drink,.
And hector when I 'm strong of it;
For I am small,
And she is tall,
And that 's the short and long of it!

O, if the bell
Would ring her knell,
I 'd make a gay ding dong of it;
For I am small,
And she is tall,
And that 's the short and long of it.

THE DUEL.

A SERIOUS BALLAD.

"Like the two Kings of Brentford smelling at one nosegay."

In Brentford town, of old renown,
There lived a Mister Bray,
Who fell in love with Lucy Bell,
And so did Mr. Clay.

To see her ride from Hammersmith,
By all it was allowed,
Such fair outsides are seldom seen,
Such Angels on a Cloud.

Said Mr. Bray to Mr. Clay,
You choose to rival me,
And court Miss Bell, but there your court
No thoroughfare shall be.

Unless you now give up your suit,
  You may repent your love ;
I who have shot a pigeon match,
  Can shoot a turtle dove.

So pray before you woo her more,
  Consider what you do ;
If you pop aught to Lucy Bell,—
  I 'll pop it into you.

Said Mr. Clay to Mr. Bray,
  Your threats I quite explode ;
One who has been a volunteer,
  Knows how to prime and load.

And so I say to you unless
  Your passion quiet keeps,
I who have shot and hit bulls' eyes,
  May chance to hit a sheep's.

Now gold is oft for silver changed,
  And that for copper red ;
But these two went away to give
  Each other change for lead.

But first they sought a friend a-piece,
  This pleasant thought to give —
When they were dead, they thus should have
  Two seconds still to live.

To measure out the ground not long
  The seconds then forbore,
And having taken one rash step
  They took a dozen more.

They next prepared each pistol-pan
  Against the deadly strife,
By putting in the prime of death
  Against the prime of life.

Now all was ready for the foes,
  But when they took their stands,
Fear made them tremble so they found
  They both were shaking hands.

Said Mr. C. to Mr. B.,
  Here one of us may fall,
And like St. Paul's Cathedral now,
  Be doomed to have a ball.

I do confess I did attach
  Misconduct to your name;
If I withdraw the charge, will then
  Your ramrod do the same?

Said Mr. B., I do agree —
  But think of Honour's Courts!
If we go off without a shot,
  There will be strange reports.

But look, the morning now is bright,
Though cloudy it begun;
Why can't we aim above, as if
We had called out the sun?

So up into the harmless air,
Their bullets they did send;
And may all other duels have
That upshot in the end!

ODE TO MR. MALTHUS.

My dear, do pull the bell,
And pull it well,
And send those noisy children all up stairs,
Now playing here like bears —
You George, and William, go into the grounds,
Charles, James, and Bob are there, — and take
your string,
Drive horses, or fly kites, or any thing,
You 're quite enough to play at hare and
hounds, —
You little May, and Caroline, and Poll,
Take each your doll,
And go, my dears, into the two-back pair,
Your sister Margaret's there —
Harriet and Grace, thank God, are both at school,
At far off Ponty Pool —

I want to read, but really can't get on —
Let the four twins, Mark, Matthew, Luke, and
John,
Go — to their nursery — go — I never can
Enjoy my Malthus among such a clan!

Oh Mr. Malthus, I agree
In every thing I read with thee!
The world 's too full, there is no doubt,
And wants a deal of thinning out, —
It 's plain — as plain as Harrow's Steeple —
And I agree with some thus far,
Who say the Queen's too popular,
That is,— she has too many people.
There are too many of all trades,
Too many bakers,
Too many every-thing-makers,
But not too many undertakers,—
Too many boys,—
Too many hobby-de-hoys,—
Too many girls, men, widows, wives and maids,—
There is a dreadful surplus to demolish,
And yet some Wrongheads,
With thick not long heads,
Poor metaphysicians!
Sign petitions
Capital punishment to abolish;
And in the face of censuses such vast ones
New hospitals contrive,
For keeping life alive,

Laying first stones, the dolts ! instead of last ones !
Others, again, in the same contrariety,
Deem that of all Humane Society
They really deserve thanks,
Because the two banks of the Serpentine,
By their design,
Are Saving Banks.
Oh ! were it given but to me to weed
The human breed,
And root out here and there some cumbering elf,
I think I could go through it,
And really do it
With profit to the world and to myself,—
For instance, the unkind among the Editors,
My debtors, those I mean to say
Who cannot or who will not pay,
And all my creditors.
These, for my own sake, I 'd destroy;
But for the world's, and every one's,
I 'd hoe up Mrs. G—'s two sons,
And Mrs. B—'s big little boy,
Called only by herself an "only joy."
As Mr. Irving's chapel 's not too full,
Himself alone I 'd pull —
But for the peace of years that have to run,
I 'd make the Lord Mayor's a perpetual station,
And put a period to rotation,
By rooting up all Aldermen but one,—
These are but hints what good might thus be done !
But ah ! I fear the public good
Is little by the public understood,—

For instance—if with flint, and steel, and tinder,
Great Swing, for once a philanthropic man,
Proposed to throw a light upon my plan,
No doubt some busy fool would hinder
His burning all the Foundling to a cinder.

Or, if the Lord Mayor, on an Easter Monday,
    That wine and bun-day,
Proposed to poison all the little Blue-coats,
Before they died by bit or sup,
Some meddling Marplot would blow up,
  Just at the moment critical,
  The economy political
Of saving their fresh yellow plush and new coats.

  Equally 'twould be undone,
  Suppose the Bishop of London,
    On that great day
    In June or May,
When all the large small family of charity,
  Brown, black, or carrotty,
Walk in their dusty parish shoes,
In too, too many two-and-twos,
To sing together till they scare the walls
    Of old St. Paul's,
Sitting in red, gray, green, blue, drab, and white,
  Some say a gratifying sight,
  Tho' I think sad — but that 's a schism —
  To witness so much pauperism —

Suppose, I say, the Bishop then, to make
In this poor overcrowded world more room,
Proposed to shake
Down that immense extinguisher, the dome —
Some humane Martin in the charity *Gal*-way
I fear would come and interfere,
Save beadle, brat, and overseer,
To walk back in their parish shoes,
In too, too many two-and-twos,
Islington — Wapping — or Pall Mall way!

Thus, people hatched from goose's egg,
Foolishly think a pest, a plague,
And in its face their doors all shut,
On hinges oiled with cajeput —
Drugging themselves with drams well spiced and cloven,
And turning pale as linen rags
At hoisting up of yellow flags,
While you and I are crying "Orange Boven!"
Why should we let precautions so absorb us,
Or trouble shipping with a quarantine —
When if I understand the thing you mean,
We ought to *import* the Cholera Morbus!

A GOOD DIRECTION.

A CERTAIN gentleman, whose yellow cheek
Proclaimed he had not been in living quite
An Anchorite —
Indeed, he scarcely ever knew a well day;
At last, by friends' advice, was led to seek
A surgeon of great note — named Aberfeldie.
A very famous Author upon Diet,
Who, better starred than Alchemists of old,
By dint of turning mercury to gold,
Had settled at his country house in quiet.

Our Patient, after some impatient rambles
Thro' Enfield roads, and Enfield lanes of brambles,
At last, to make inquiry had the *nous*,—
"Here, my good man,
Just tell me if you can,
Pray which is Mr. Aberfeldie's house?"
The man thus stopped — perusing for a while
The yellow visage of the man of bile,
At last made answer, with a broadish grin:
"Why, turn to right — and left — and right agin,
The road 's direct — you cannot fail to go it."
"But stop! my worthy fellow! — one word more —
From other houses how am I to know it!"

"How! — why you'll see *blue pillars* at the door!"

THERE 'S NO ROMANCE IN THAT!

"So while I fondly imagined we were deceiving my relations, and flattered myself that I should outwit and incense them all; behold, my hopes are to be crushed at once, by my aunt's consent and approbation, and I am myself the only dupe.. But here, Sir,—here is the picture!"

LYDIA LANGUISH.

O DAYS of old, O days of Knights,
Of tourneys and of tilts,
When love was balked and valor stalked
On high heroic stilts—
Where are ye gone?—adventures cease,
The world gets tame and flat,—
We 've nothing now but New Police—
There 's no romance in that!

I wish I ne'er had learned to read,
Or Radcliffe how to write;
That Scott had been a boor on Tweed,
And Lewis cloister'd quite!
Would I had never drunk so deep
Of dear Miss Porter's vat;
I only turn to life, and weep—
There 's no Romance in that!

No Bandits lurk—no turbaned Turk
To Tunis bears me off—
I hear no noises in the night
Except my mother's cough,—

No Bleeding Spectre haunts the house,
No shape,—but owl or bat,
Come flitting after moth or mouse,—
There 's no Romance in that!

I have not any grief profound,
Or secrets to confess,
My story would not fetch a pound
For A. K. Newman's press;
Instead of looking thin and pale,
I 'm growing red and fat,
As if I lived on beef and ale—
There 's no Romance in that!

It's very hard, by land or sea
Some strange event I court,
But nothing ever comes to me
That 's worth a pen's report:
It really made my temper chafe,
Each coast that I was at,
I vowed, and railed, and came home safe,—
There 's no Romance in that!

The only time I had a chance
At Brighton one fine day,
My chestnut mare began to prance,
Took fright, and ran away;
Alas! no Captain of the Tenth
To stop my steed came pat;
A Butcher caught the rein at length,—
There 's no Romance in that!

Love — even love — goes smoothly on
A railway sort of track —
No flinty sire, no jealous Don!
No hearts upon the rack;
No Polydore, no Theodore —
His ugly name is Mat,
Plain Matthew Pratt and nothing more —
There's no Romance in that!

He is not dark, he is not tall, —
His forehead's rather low,
He is not pensive — not at all,
But smiles his teeth to show;
He comes from Wales and yet in size
Is really but a sprat;
With sandy hair and grayish eyes —
There's no Romance in that!

He wears no plumes or Spanish cloaks,
Or long-sword hanging down;
He dresses much like other folks,
And commonly in brown;
His collar he will not discard,
Or give up his cravat,
Lord Byron-like — he's not a Bard —
There's no Romance in that!

He's rather bald, his sight is weak,
He's deaf in either drum;
Without a lisp he cannot speak,

But then — he 's worth a plum.
He talks of stocks and three per cents.
By way of private chat,
Of Spanish Bonds, and shares, and rents—
There 's no Romance in that!

I sing — no matter what I sing,
Di Tanti — or Crudel,
Tom Bowling, or God save the King,
Di piacer — All 's well;
He knows no more about a voice
For singing than a gnat —
And as to Music "has no choice"—
There 's no Romance in that!

Of light guitar I cannot boast,
He never serenades;
He writes, and sends it by the post,
He doesn't bribe the maids:
No stealth, no hempen ladder — no!
He comes with loud rat-tat,
That startles half of Bedford Row —
There 's no Romance in that!

He comes at nine in time to choose
His coffee — just two cups,
And talks with Pa about the news,
Repeats debates, and sups.
John helps him with his coat aright,
And Jenkins hands his hat;

My lover bows, and says good night —
There 's no Romance in that!

I 've long had Pa's and Ma's consent,
My Aunt she quite approves,
My Brother wishes joy from Kent,
None try to thwart our loves;
On Tuesday reverend Mr. Mace
Will make me Mrs. Pratt,
Of Number Twenty, Sussex Place —
There 's no Romance in that!

A WATERLOO BALLAD.

To Waterloo, with sad ado,
  And many a sigh and groan,
Amongst the dead, came Patty Head,
  To look for Peter Stone.

"O prithee tell, good sentinel,
  If I shall find him here?
I'm come to weep upon his corse,
  My Ninety-Second dear!

"Into our town a sergeant came
  With ribbons all so fine,
A-flaunting in his cap — alas!
  His bow enlisted mine!

"They taught him how to turn his toes,
And stand as stiff as starch;
I thought that it was love and May,
But it was love and March!

"A sorry March indeed to leave
The friends he might have kep, —
No March of Intellect it was,
But quite a foolish step.

"O prithee tell, good sentinel,
If hereabout he lies?
I want a corpse with reddish hair,
And very sweet blue eyes."

Her sorrow on the sentinel
Appeared to deeply strike: —
"Walk in," he said, "among the dead,
And pick out which you like."

And soon she picked out Peter Stone,
Half turned into a corse;
A cannon was his bolster, and
His mattress was a horse.

"O Peter Stone, O Peter Stone,
Lord, here has been a skrimmage!
What have they done to your poor breast
That used to hold my image?"

"O Patty Head, O Patty Head,
You 're come to my last kissing;
Before I'm set in the Gazette
As wounded, dead, and missing!

"Alas! a splinter of a shell
Right in my stomach sticks;
French mortars don't agree so well
With stomachs as French bricks.

"This very night a merry dance
At Brussels was to be;—
Instead of opening a ball,
A ball has opened me.

"Its billet every bullet has,
And well it does fulfil it;—
I wish mine hadn't come so straight,
But been a 'crooked billet.'

"And then there came a cuirassier
And cut me on the chest;—
He had no pity in his heart,
For he had *steeled his breast.*

"Next thing a lancer, with his lance,
Began to thrust away;
I called for quarter, but, alas!
It was not Quarter-day.

"He ran his spear right through my arm,
Just here above the joint: —
O Patty dear, it was no joke,
Although it had a point.

"With loss of blood I fainted off,
As dead as women do —
But soon by charging over me,
The *Coldstream* brought me to.

"With kicks and cuts, and balls and blows,
I throb and ache all over;
I 'm quite convinced the field of Mars
Is not a field of clover!

"O why did I a soldier turn
For any royal Guelph?
I might have been a butcher, and
In business for myself!

"O why did I the bounty take
(And here he gasped for breath)
My shillingsworth of list is nailed
Upon the door of death!

"Without a coffin I shall lie
And sleep my sleep eternal:
Not ev'n a *shell* — my only chance
Of being made a *Kernel!*

"O Patty dear, our wedding bells
Will never ring at Chester!
Here I must lie in Honour's bed,
That isn't worth a *tester!*

"Farewell, my regimental mates,
With whom I used to dress!
My corps is changed, and I am now,
In quite another mess.

"Farewell, my Patty dear, I have
No dying consolations,
Except, when I am dead, you'll go
And see th' Illuminations."

SHOOTING PAINS.

"The charge is prepared." — MACHEATH.

IF I shoot any more I'll be shot,
For ill-luck seems determined to star me,
I have marched the whole day
With a gun, — for no pay —
Zounds, I'd better have been in the army!

What matters Sir Christopher's leave ;
To his manor I 'm sorry I came yet !
With confidence fraught,
My two pointers I brought,
But we are not a point towards game yet !

And that gamekeeper too, with advice !
Of my course he has been a nice chalker,
Not far, were his words,
I could go without birds :
If my legs could cry out, they 'd cry " Walker ! "

Not Hawker could find out a flaw,—
My appointments are modern and Mantony,
And I 've brought my own man,
To mark down all he can,
But I can't find a mark for my Antony !

The partridges,— where can they lie ?
I have promised a leash to Miss Jervas,
As the least I could do ;
But without even two
To brace me,— I 'm getting quite nervous !

To the pheasants — how well they 're preserved !
My sport 's not a jot more beholden,
As the birds are so shy,
For my friends I must buy,
And so send " silver pheasants and golden."

I have tried ev'ry form for a hare,
Every patch, every furze that could shroud her,
    With toil unrelaxed,
    Till my patience is taxed,
But I cannot be taxed for hare-powder.

I 've been roaming for hours in three flats
In the hope of a snipe for a snap at;
    But still vainly I court
    The percussioning sport,
I find nothing for "setting my cap at!"

A woodcock,— this month is the time,—
Right and left I 've made ready my lock for,
    With well-loaded double,
    But spite of my trouble,
Neither barrel can I find a cock for!

A rabbit I should not despise,
But they lurk in their burrows so lowly
    This day 's the eleventh,
    It is not the seventh,
But they seem to be keeping it hole-y.

For a mallard I 've waded the marsh,
And haunted each pool, and each lake — oh
    Mine is not the luck,
    To obtain thee, O Duck,
Or to doom thee, O Drake, like a Draco!

For a field-fare I 've fared far a-field,
Large or small I am never to sack bird,
Not a thrush is so kind
As to fly, and I find
I may whistle myself for a black-bird!

I am angry, I 'm hungry, I 'm dry,
Disappointed, and sullen, and goaded,
And so weary an elf,
I am sick of myself,
And with Number One seem overloaded.

As well one might beat round St. Paul's,
And look out for a cock or a hen there;
I have searched round and round
All the Baronet's ground,
But Sir Christopher hasn't a wren there!

Joyce may talk of his excellent caps,
But for nightcaps they set me desiring,
And it 's really too bad,
Not a shot I have had
With Hall's Powder, renowned for "quick firing."

If this is what people call sport,
Oh! of sporting I can't have a high sense,
And there still remains one
More mischance on my gun —
"Fined for shooting without any license."

THE BOY AT THE NORE.

"Alone I did it! — Boy!" — CORIOLANUS.

I SAY, little Boy at the Nore,
  Do you come from the small Isle of Man?
Why, your history a mystery must be,—
  Come tell us as much as you can,
          Little Boy at the Nore!

You live it seems wholly on water,
  Which your Gambier calls living in clover;—
But how comes it, if that is the case,
  You 're eternally half seas over,—
          Little Boy at the Nore?

While you ride — while you dance — while you
    float —
  Never mind your imperfect orthography;—
But give us as well as you can,
  Your watery auto-biography,
          Little Boy at the Nore!

LITTLE BOY AT THE NORE LOQUITUR.

I 'm the tight little Boy at the Nore,
  In a sort of sea negus I dwells;

Half and half 'twixt salt water and Port,
  I 'm reckoned the first of the swells —
                  I 'm the Boy at the Nore!

I lives with my toes to the flounders,
  And watches through long days and nights;
Yet, cruelly eager, men look —
  To catch the first glimpse of my lights —
                  I 'm the Boy at the Nore.

I never gets cold in the head,
  So my life on salt water is sweet,—
I think I owes much of my health,
  To being well used to wet feet —
                  As the Boy at the Nore.

There 's one thing, I 'm never in debt:
  Nay! — I liquidates more than I *oughter;* *
So the man to beat Cits as goes by,
  In keeping the head above water,
                  Is the Boy at the Nore.

I 've seen a good deal of distress,
  Lots of Breakers in Ocean's Gazette;
They should do as I do — rise o'er all;
  Ay, a good floating capital get,
                  Like the Boy at the Nore!

* A word caught from some American Trader in passing.

I 'm a'ter the sailor's own heart,
  And cheers him, in deep water rolling ;
And the friend of all friends to Jack Junk,
  Ben Backstay, Tom Pipes, and Tom Bowling.
        Is the Boy at the Nore !

Could I e'er but grow up, I 'd be off
  For a week to make love with my wheedles ;
If the tight little Boy at the Nore
  Could but catch a nice girl at the Needles,
        We 'd have *two* at the Nore !

They thinks little of sizes on water,
  On big waves the tiny one skulks,—
While the river has Men of War on it —
  Yes — the Thames is oppressed with Great
    Hulks.
        And the Boy's at the Nore !

But I 've done — for the water is heaving
  Round my body, as though it would sink it !
And I 've been so long pitching and tossing,
  That sea-sick — you 'd hardly now think it —
        Is the Boy at the Nore !

ODE TO ST. SWITHIN.

"The rain it raineth every day."

THE Dawn is overcast, the morning lowers,
On ev'ry window-frame hang beaded damps
Like rows of small illumination lamps,
To celebrate the Jubilee of Showers!
A constant sprinkle patters from all leaves,
The very Dryads are not dry, but soppers,
  And from the Houses' eaves
  Tumble eaves-droppers.

The hundred clerks that live along the street,
Bondsmen to mercantile and city schemers,
With squashing, sloshing, and galloshing feet,
Go paddling, paddling, through the wet, like
    steamers,
Each hurrying to earn the daily stipend —
Umbrellas pass of every shade of green,
And now and then a crimson one is seen,
  Like an Umbrella *ripened.*

  Over the way a wagon
Stands with six smoking horses, shrinking, blink-
    ing,

While in the George and Dragon
The man is keeping himself dry — and drinking!
The Butcher's boy skulks underneath his tray,
Hats shine — shoes don't — and down droop
collars,
And one blue Parasol cries all the way
To school, in company with four small scholars!

Unhappy is the man to-day who rides,
Making his journey sloppier, not shorter;
Ay, there they go, a dozen of outsides,
Performing on "a Stage with real water!"
A dripping pauper crawls along the way,
The only real willing out-of-doorer,
And says, or seems to say,
"Well, I am poor enough — but here's a *pourer!*"

The scene in water colors thus I paint,
Is your own Festival, you Sloppy Saint!
Mother of all the Family of Rainers!
Saint of the Soakers!
Making all people croakers,
Like frogs in swampy marshes, and complainers!
And why you mizzle forty days together,
Giving the earth your water-soup to sup,
I marvel — Why such wet, mysterious weather?
I wish you 'd *clear it up!*

Why cast such cruel dampers
On pretty Pic Nics, and against all wishes

Set the cold ducks a-swimming in the hampers,
And volunteer, unasked, to wash the dishes?
Why drive the Nymphs from the selected spot,
  To cling like lady-birds around a tree —
  Why spoil a Gipsy party at their tea,
By throwing your cold water upon hot?

Cannot a rural maiden, or a man,
Seek Hornsey-Wood by invitation, sipping
  Their green with Pan,
But souse you come, and show their Pan all
    dripping!
Why upon snow-white tablecloths and sheets,
That do not wait, or want a second washing,
      Come squashing?
Why task yourself to lay the dust in streets,
As if there were no Water-Cart contractors,
No pot-boys spilling beer, no shop-boys ruddy
  Spooning out puddles muddy,
Milkmaids, and other slopping benefactors!

A Queen you are, raining in your own right,
Yet oh! how little flattered by report!
  Even by those that seek the Court,
Pelted with every term of spleen and spite.
Folks rail and swear at you in every place;
They say you are a creature of no bowel;
They say you 're always washing Nature's face,
  And that you then supply her,
      With nothing drier,

Than some old wringing cloud by way of towel!
The whole town wants you ducked, just as you
 duck it,
They wish you on your own mud porridge
 suppered,
They hope that you may kick your own big
 bucket,
Or in your water-butt go souse! heels up'ard!
They are, in short, so weary of your drizzle,
They 'd spill the water in your veins to stop it —
Be warned! You are too partial to a mizzle —
 Pray *drop it!*

THE SCHOOLMASTER'S MOTTO.

"The Admiral compelled them all to strike." — Life of Nelson.

Hush! silence in School — not a noise!
You shall soon see there 's nothing to jeer at,
Master Marsh, most audacious of boys!
Come! — "Palmam qui meruit ferat!"

So this morn in the midst of the Psalm,
The Miss Siffkins's school you must leer at,
You 're complained of — Sir! hold out your
 palm —
There! — "Palmam qui meruit ferat!"

You wilful young rebel, and dunce!
This offence all your sins shall appear at,
You shall have a good caning at once —
There! — "Palmam qui meruit ferat!"

You are backward, you know, in each verb,
And your pronouns you are not more clear at,
But you 're forward enough to disturb —
There! — "Palmam qui meruit ferat!"

You said Master Twigg stole the plums,
When the orchard he never was near at,
I 'll not punish wrong fingers or thumbs —
There! — "Palmam qui meruit ferat!"

You make Master Taylor your butt,
And this morning his face you threw beer at,
And you struck him — do *you* like a cut?
There! — "Palmam qui meruit ferat!"

Little Biddle you likewise distress,
You are always his hair, or his ear at,—
He 's my *Opt*, Sir, and you are my *Pess*:
There! — "Palmam qui meruit ferat!"

Then you had a pitched fight with young Rouse,
An offence I am always severe at!
You discredit to Cicero-House!
There! — "Palmam qui meruit ferat!"

You have made too a plot in the night,
To run off from the school that you rear at!
Come, your other hand, now, Sir,— the right,
There! — "Palmam qui meruit ferat!"

I 'll teach you to draw, you young dog!
Such pictures as I 'm looking here at!
"Old Mounseer making soup of a frog,"
There! — "Palmam qui meruit ferat!"

You have run up a bill at a shop,
That in paying you 'll be a whole year at —
You 've but twopence a week, Sir, to stop!
There! — "Palmam qui meruit ferat!"

Then at dinner you 're quite cock-a-hoop,
And the soup you are certain to sneer at —
I have sipped it — it 's very good soup —
There! — "Palmam qui meruit ferat!"

T'other day when I fell o'er the form,
Was my tumble a thing, Sir, to cheer at?
Well for you that my temper 's not warm —
There! — "Palmam qui meruit ferat!"

Why, you rascal! you insolent brat!
All my talking you don't shed a tear at,
There — take that, Sir! and that! that! and that!
There! — "Palmam qui meruit ferat!"

THE SUPPER SUPERSTITION.

A PATHETIC BALLAD.

"Oh flesh, flesh, how art thou fishified!" — MERCUTIO.

I.

'Twas twelve o'clock by Chelsea chimes,
When all in hungry trim,
Good Mister Jupp sat down to sup
With wife, and Kate, and Jim.

II.

Said he, "Upon this dainty cod
How bravely I shall sup," —
When, whiter than the tablecloth,
A GHOST came rising up!

III.

"O, father dear, O, mother dear,
Dear Kate, and brother Jim,—
You know when some one went to sea,—
Don't cry — but I am him!

IV.

"You hope some day with fond embrace
To greet your absent Jack,
But oh, I am come here to say
I 'm never coming back!

V.

"From Alexandria we set sail,
With corn, and oil, and figs,
But steering 'too much Sow,' we struck
Upon the Sow and Pigs!

VI.

"The Ship we pumped till we could see
Old England from the tops;
When down she went with all our hands,
Right in the Channel's Chops.

VII.

"Just give a look in Norey's chart,
The very place it tells;
I think it says twelve fathom deep,
Clay bottom, mixed with shells.

VIII.

"Well there we are till 'hands aloft,'
We have at last a call;
The pug I had for brother Jim,
Kate's parrot too, and all.

IX.

"But oh, my spirit cannot rest,
In Davy Jones's sod,
Till I 've appeared to you and said,—
Don't sup on that 'ere Cod!

X.

"You live on land, and little think
What passes in the sea;
Last Sunday week, at 2 P. M.
That Cod was picking me!

XI.

"Those oysters too, that look so plump,
And seem so nicely done,
They put my corpse in many shells,
Instead of only one.

XII.

"O, do not eat those oysters then,
And do not touch the shrimps;
When I was in my briny grave,
They sucked my blood like imps!

XIII.

"Don't eat what brutes would never eat,
The brutes I used to pat,
They 'll know the smell they used to smell,
Just try the dog and cat!"

XIV.

The Spirit fled — they wept his fate,
And cried, Alack, alack!
At last up started brother Jim,
"Let 's try if Jack was Jack!"

XV.

They called the Dog, they called the Cat,
And little Kitten too,
And down they put the Cod and sauce,
To see what brutes would do.

XVI.

Old Tray licked all the oysters up,
Puss never stood at crimps,
But munched the Cod,— and little Kit
Quite feasted on the shrimps!

XVII.

The thing was odd, and minus Cod
And sauce, they stood like posts;
O, prudent folks, for fear of hoax,
Put no belief in Ghosts!

A STORM AT HASTINGS,

AND THE LITTLE UNKNOWN.

'Twas August — Hastings every day was filling —
Hastings, that "greenest spot on memory's waste!"
With crowds of idlers willing or unwilling
To be bedipped — be noticed — or be braced,
And all things rose a penny in a shilling.
Meanwhile, from window and from door, in haste
"Accommodation bills" kept coming down,
Gladding "the world of letters" in that town.

Each day poured in new coach-fulls of new cits,
Flying from London smoke and dust annoying,
Unmarried Misses hoping to make hits,
And new-wed couples fresh from Tunbridge toying,
Lacemen and placemen, ministers and wits,
And quakers of both sexes, much enjoying
A morning's reading by the ocean's rim,
That sect delighting in the sea's broad brim.

And lo! amongst all these appeared a creature,
So small, he almost might a twin have been

With Miss Crachami — dwarfish quite in stature,
Yet well proportioned — neither fat nor lean,
His face of marvellously pleasant feature,
So short and sweet a man was never seen —
All thought him charming at the first beginning —
Alas, ere long they found him far too winning!

He seemed in love with chance — and chance repaid
His ardent passion with her fondest smile,
The sunshine of good luck, without a shade,
He staked and won — and won and staked — the bile
It stirred of many a man and many a maid,
To see at every venture how that vile [too —
Small gambler snatched — and how he won them
A living Pam, omnipotent at loo!

Miss Wiggins set her heart upon a box,
'Twas handsome, rosewood, and inlaid with brass,
And dreamt three times she garnished it with stocks
Of needles, silks, and cottons — but alas!
She lost it wide awake. — We thought Miss Cox
Was lucky — but she saw three caddies pass
To that small imp; — no living luck could loo him!
Sir Stamford would have lost his Raffles to him!

And so he climbed — and rode, and won — and walked,

The wondrous topic of the curious swarm
That haunted the Parade. Many were balked
Of notoriety by that small form
Pacing it up and down : — some even talked
Of ducking him — when lo ! a dismal storm
Stepped in — one Friday, at the close of day —
And every head was turned another way —

Watching the grander guest. It seemed to rise
Bulky and slow upon the southern brink
Of the horizon — fanned by sultry sighs —
So black and threatening, I cannot think
Of any simile, except the skies
Miss Wiggins sometimes *shades* in Indian ink —
Miss-shapen blotches of such heavy vapour,
They seem a deal more solid than her paper.

As for the sea, it did not fret, and rave,
And tear its waves to tatters, and so dash on
The stony-hearted beach ; — some bards would
have
It always rampant, in that idle fashion,—
Whereas the waves rolled in, subdued and grave,
Like schoolboys, when the master 's in a passion,
Who meekly settle in and take their places,
With a very quiet awe on all their faces.

Some love to draw the ocean with a head,
Like troubled table-beer,— and make it bounce,
And froth, and roar, and fling,— but this, I 've
said,

Surged in scarce rougher than a lady's flounce: —
But then, a grander contrast thus it bred
With the wild welkin, seeming to pronounce
Something more awful in the serious ear,
As one would whisper that a lion 's near —

Who just begins to roar: so the hoarse thunder
Growled long — but low — a prelude note of
 death,
As if the stifling clouds yet kept it under,
But still it muttered to the sea beneath
Such a continued peal, as made us wonder
It did not pause more oft to take its breath,
Whilst we were panting with the sultry weather,
And hardly cared to wed two words together,

But watched the surly advent of the storm,
Much as the brown-cheeked planters of Barbadoes
Must watch a rising of the Negro swarm: —
Meantime it steered, like Odin's old Armadas,
Right on our coast; — a dismal, coal-black
 form; —
Many proud gaits were quelled — and all bra-
 vadoes
Of folly ceased — and sundry idle jokers
Went home to cover up their tongs and pokers.

So fierce the lightning flashed.— In all their days
The oldest smugglers had not seen such flashing
And they are used to many a pretty blaze,

To keep their Hollands from an awkward clashing
With hostile cutters in our creeks and bays: —
And truly one could think without much lashing
The fancy, that those coasting clouds so awful
And black, were fraught with spirits as unlawful.

The gay Parade grew thin — all the fair crowd
Vanished — as if they knew their own attractions, —
For now the lightning through a near hand cloud
Began to make some very crooked fractions —
Only some few remained that were not cowed,
A few rough sailors, who had been in actions,
And sundry boatmen, that with quick yeo's,
Lest it should *blow*, — were pulling up the *Rose:*

(No flower, but a boat) — some more hauling
The *Regent* by the head: — another crew
With that same cry peculiar to their *calling* —
Were heaving up the *Hope:* — and as they knew
The very gods themselves oft get a mauling
In their own realms, the seamen wisely drew
The *Neptune* rather higher on the beach,
That he might lie beyond his billows' reach.

And now the storm, with its despotic power
Had all usurped the azure of the skies,
Making our daylight darker by an hour,
And some few drops — of an unusual size —

Few and distinct — scarce twenty to the shower,
Fell like huge tear-drops from a Giant's eyes —
But then this sprinkle thickened in a trice
And rained much *harder* — in good solid ice.

Oh! for a very storm of words to show
How this fierce crash of hail came rushing o'er us!
Handel would make the gusty organs blow
Grandly, and a rich storm in music score us; —
But ev'n his music seemed composed and low,
When we were *handled* by this Hailstone Chorus;
Whilst thunder rumbled, with its awful sound,
And frozen comfits rolled along the ground —

As big as bullets: — Lord! how they did batter
Our crazy tiles: — And now the lightning flashed
Alternate with the dark, until the latter
Was rarest of the two: — the gust too dashed
So terribly, I thought the hail must shatter
Some panes, — and so it did, — and first it smashed
The very square where I had chose my station
To watch the general illumination.

Another, and another, still came in,
And fell in jingling ruin at my feet,
Making transparent holes that let me win
Some samples of the storm: — Oh! it was sweet
To think I had a shelter for my skin,
Culling them through these "loopholes of retreat" —

Which in a little we began to glaze —
Chiefly with a jacktowel and some baize!

By which, the cloud had passed o'erhead, but
played
Its crooked fires in constant flashes still,
Just in our rear, as though it had arrayed
Its heavy batteries at Fairlight Mill,
So that it lit the town, and grandly made
The rugged features of the Castle Hill
Leap, like a birth, from chaos, into light,
And then relapse into the gloomy night —

As parcel of the cloud; — the clouds themselves,
Like monstrous crags and summits everlasting,
Piled each on each in most gigantic shelves,
That Milton's devils were engaged in blasting.—
We could e'en fancy Satan and his elves
Busy upon those crags, and ever casting [sound
Huge fragments loose,— and that we *felt* the
They made in falling to the startled ground.

And so the tempest scowled away,— and soon
Timidly shining through its skirts of jet,
We saw the rim of the pacific moon,
Like a bright fish entangled in a net,
Flashing its silver sides,— how sweet a boon,
Seemed her sweet light, as though it would beget,
With that fair smile, a calm upon the seas —
Peace in the sky — and coolness in the breeze!

Meantime the hail had ceased: — and all the
brood
Of glaziers stole abroad to count their gains;—
At every window, there were maids who stood
Lamenting o'er the glass's small remains,—
Or with coarse linens made the fractions good,
Stanching the wind in all the wounded panes,—
Or, holding candles to the panes, in doubt:
The wind resolved — blowing the candles out.

No house was whole that had a southern front,—
No greenhouse but the same mishap befell; —
Bow-windows and *bell*-glasses bore the brunt,—
No sex in glass was spared !—— For those who
dwell
On each hill-side, you might have swam a punt
In any of their parlors; — Mrs. Snell
Was slopped out of her seat,— and Mr. Hitchin
Had a *flower*-garden washed into a *Kitchen*.

But still the sea was mild, and quite disclaimed
The recent violence.—Each after each
The gentle waves a gentle murmur framed,
Tapping, like Woodpeckers, the hollow beach.
Howbeit his *weather eye* the seaman aimed
Across the calm, and hinted by his speech
A gale next morning — and when morning
broke,
There was a gale — "quite equal to bespoke."

Before high water — (it were better far
To christen it not *water* then but *waiter*,
For then the tide is *serving at the bar*)
Rose such a swell — I never saw one greater!
Black, jagged billows rearing up in war
Like ragged roaring bears against the baiter,
With lots of froth upon the shingle shed,
Like stout poured out with a fine *beachy head.*

No open boat was open to a fare,
Or launched that morn on seven-shilling trips,
No bathing woman waded — none would dare
A dipping in the wave — but waived their dips,
No seagull ventured on the stormy air,
And all the dreary coast was clear of ships;
For two *lea shores* upon the river Lea
Are not so perilous as one at sea.

Awe-struck we sat, and gazed upon the scene
Before us in such horrid hurly-burly,—
A boiling ocean of mixed black and green,
A sky of copper color, grim and surly,—
When lo, in that vast hollow scooped between
Two rolling Alps of water,—white and curly!
We saw a pair of little arms a-skimming,
Much like a first or last attempt at swimming!

Sometimes a hand — sometimes a little shoe —
Sometimes a skirt — sometimes a hank of hair

Just like a dabbled seaweed rose to view,
Sometimes a knee, sometimes a back was bare —
At last a frightful summerset he threw
Right on the shingles. Any one could swear
The lad was dead — without a chance of perjury,
And battered by the surge beyond all surgery!

However we snatched up the corse thus thrown,
Intending, Christian-like, to sod and turf it,
And after venting Pity's sigh and groan,
Then Curiosity began with *her* fit;
And lo! the features of the Small Unknown!
'Twas he that of the surf had had this surfeit! —
And in his fob, the cause of late monopolies,
We found a contract signed with Mephistophiles!

A bond of blood, whereby the sinner gave
His forfeit soul to Satan in reversion,
Providing in this world he was to have
A lordship over luck, by whose exertion
He might control the course of cards, and brave
All throws of dice,—but on a sea excursion
The juggling Demon, in his usual vein,
Seized the last cast — and *Nicked* him in the
main!

LINES

TO A LADY ON HER DEPARTURE FOR INDIA.

Go where the waves run rather Holborn-hilly,
And tempests make a soda-water sea,
Almost as rough as our rough Piccadilly,
And think of me!

Go where the mild Madeira ripens *her* juice,—
A wine more praised than it deserves to be!
Go pass the Cape, just capable of ver-juice,
And think of me!

Go where the Tiger in the darkness prowleth,
Making a midnight meal of he and she;
Go where the Lion in his hunger howleth,
And think of me!

Go where the serpent dangerously coileth,
Or lies along at full length like a tree,
Go where the Suttee in her own soot broileth,
And think of me!

Go where with human notes the Parrot dealeth
In mono-*polly*-logue with tongue as free,
And like a woman, all she can revealeth,
And think of me!

Go to the land of muslin and nankeening,
And parasols of straw where hats should be,
Go to the land of slaves and palankeening,
And think of me!

Go to the land of Jungles and of vast hills,
And tall bamboos — may none *bamboozle* thee!
Go gaze upon their Elephants and Castles,
And think of me!

Go where a cook must always be a currier,
And parch the peppered palate like a pea,
Go where the fierce mosquito is a worrier,
And think of me!

Go where the maiden on a marriage plan goes,
Consigned for wedlock to Calcutta's quay,
Where woman goes for mart, the same as mangoes,
And think of me!

Go where the sun is very hot and fervent,
Go to the land of pagod and rupee,
Where every black will be your slave and servant,
And think of me!

HUGGINS AND DUGGINS.

A PASTORAL AFTER POPE.

Two swains or clowns — but call them swains —
While keeping flocks on Salisbury Plains,
For all that tend on sheep as drovers,
Are turned to songsters, or to lovers,
Each of the lass he called his dear,
Began to carol loud and clear.
First Huggins sang, and Duggins then,
In the way of ancient shepherd men;
Who thus alternate hitched in song,
"All things by turns, and nothing long."

HUGGINS.

Of all the girls about our place,
There 's one beats all in form and face;
Search through all Great and Little Bumpstead,
You 'll only find one Peggy Plumstead.

DUGGINS.

To groves and streams I tell my flame,
I make the cliffs repeat her name:
When I 'm inspired by gills and noggins,
The rocks reëcho Sally Hoggins!

HUGGINS.

When I am walking in the grove,
I think of Peggy as I rove.
I 'd carve her name on every tree,
But I don't know my A, B, C.

DUGGINS.

Whether I walk in hill or valley,
I think of nothing else but Sally.
I 'd sing her praise, but I can sing
No song, except "God save the King."

HUGGINS.

My Peggy does all nymphs excel,
And all confess she bears the bell,—
Where'er she goes swains flock together,
Like sheep that follow the bellwether.

DUGGINS.

Sally is tall and not too straight,—
Those very poplar shapes I hate;
But something twisted like an S,—
A crook becomes a shepherdess.

HUGGINS.

When Peggy's dog her arms emprison,
I often wish my lot was hisn;
How often I should stand and turn,
To get a pat from hands like hern.

DUGGINS.

I tell Sall's lambs how blest they be,
To stand about and stare at she;
But when I look, she turns and shies,
And won't bear none but their sheep's-eyes!

HUGGINS.

Love goes with Peggy where she goes,—
Beneath her smile the garden grows;
Potatoes spring, and cabbage starts,
'Tatoes have eyes, and cabbage hearts!

DUGGINS.

Where Sally goes it 's always Spring,
Her presence brightens every thing;
The sun smiles bright, but where her grin is,
It makes brass farthings look like guineas.

HUGGINS.

For Peggy I can have no joy,
She 's sometimes kind, and sometimes coy,
And keeps me, by her wayward tricks,
As comfortless as sheep with ticks.

DUGGINS.

Sally is ripe as June or May,
And yet as cold as Christmas day;
For when she 's asked to change her lot,
Lamb's wool,— but Sally, she wool not.

HUGGINS.

Only with Peggy and with health,
I 'd never wish for state or wealth ;
Talking of having health and more pence,
I 'd drink her health if I had fourpence.

DUGGINS.

Oh, how that day would seem to shine,
If Sally's banns were read with mine ;
She cries, when such a wish I carry,
" Marry come up ! " but will not marry.

DOMESTIC DIDACTICS.

BY A FOOTMAN.

THE BROKEN DISH.

WHAT 's life but full of care and doubt,
With all its fine humanities,
With parasols we walk about,
Long pigtails and such vanities.

We plant pomegranate trees and things,
And go in gardens sporting,
With toys and fans of peacock's wings,
To painted ladies courting.

We gather flowers of every hue,
And fish in boats for fishes,
Build summer-houses painted blue,—
But life 's as frail as dishes.

Walking about their groves of trees,
Blue bridges and blue rivers,
How little thought them two Chinese,
They 'd both be smashed to shivers.

ODE TO PEACE.

WRITTEN ON THE NIGHT OF MY MISTRESS'S GRAND ROUT.

Oh Peace! oh come with me and dwell —
But stop, for there 's the bell.
Oh Peace! for thee I go and sit in churches,
On Wednesday, when there 's very few
In loft or pew —
Another ring, the tarts are come from Birch's.
Oh Peace! for thee I have avoided marriage —
Hush! there 's a carriage.
Oh Peace! thou art the best of earthly goods —
The five Miss Woods.
Oh Peace! thou art the Goddess I adore —
There come some more.
Oh Peace! thou child of solitude and quiet —
That 's Lord Drum's footman, for he loves a riot.

Oh Peace!
Knocks will not cease.
Oh Peace! thou wert for human comfort planned —
That 's Weippert's band.
Oh Peace! how glad I welcome thy approaches —
I hear the sound of coaches.
Oh Peace! oh Peace! — another carriage stops —
It 's early for the Blenkinsops.

Oh Peace! with thee I love to wander,
But wait till I have showed up Lady Squander,
And now I 've seen her up the stair,
Oh Peace! — but here comes Captain Hare.
Oh Peace! thou art the slumber of the mind,
Untroubled, calm and quiet, and unbroken,—
If that is Alderman Guzzle from Portsoken,
Alderman Gobble won't be far behind;
Oh Peace! serene in worldly shyness,—
Make way there for his Serene Highness!

Oh Peace! if you do not disdain
To dwell amongst the menial train,
I have a silent place, and lone,
That you and I may call our own;
Where tumult never makes an entry —
Susan, what business have you in my pantry?

Oh Peace! but there is Major Monk,
At variance with his wife — Oh Peace!

And that great German, Vander Trunk,
And that great talker, Miss Apreece;
Oh Peace! so dear to poets' quills —
They 're just beginning their quadrilles —
Oh Peace! our greatest renovator; —
I wonder where I put my waiter —
Oh Peace! — but here my Ode I 'll cease;
I have no peace to write of Peace.

A FEW LINES ON COMPLETING FORTY-SEVEN.

When I reflect with serious sense,
While years and years run on,
How soon I may be summoned hence —
There 's cook a-calling John.

Our lives are built so frail and poor,
On sand and not on rocks,
We 're hourly standing at Death's door —
There 's some one double-knocks.

All human days have settled terms,
Our fates we cannot force;
This flesh of mine will feed the worms —
They 're come to lunch of course.

And when my body 's turned to clay,
And dear friends hear my knell,

O let them give a sigh and say —
I hear the upstairs bell.

TO MARY HOUSEMAID.

ON VALENTINE'S DAY.

MARY, you know I 've no love-nonsense,
And, though I pen on such a day,
I don't mean flirting, on my conscience,
Or writing in the courting way.

Though Beauty hasn't formed your feature,
It saves you, perhaps, from being vain,
And many a poor unhappy creature
May wish that she was half as plain.

Your virtues would not rise an inch,
Although your shape was two foot taller,
And wisely you let others pinch
Great waists and feet to make them smaller.

You never try to spare your hands
From getting red by household duty
But, doing all that it commands,
Their coarseness is a moral beauty.

Let Susan flourish her fair arms
And at your odd legs sneer and scoff,
But let her laugh, for you have charms
That nobody knows nothing of.

PAIN IN A PLEASURE BOAT.

A SEA ECLOGUE.

"I apprehend you!" — SCHOOL OF REFORM.

BOATMAN.

SHOVE off there! — ship the rudder, Bill — cast off! she 's under way!

MRS. F.

She 's under what? — I hope she 's not! good gracious, what a spray!

BOATMAN.

Run out the jib, and rig the boom! keep clear of those two brigs!

MRS. F.

I hope they don't intend some joke by running of their rigs!

BOATMAN.

Bill, shift them bags of ballast aft — she 's rather out of trim!

MRS. F.

Great bags of stones! they 're pretty things to help a boat to swim!

BOATMAN.

The wind is fresh — if she don't scud, it 's not the breeze's fault!

MRS. F.

Wind fresh, indeed, I never felt the air so full of salt!

BOATMAN.

That schooner, Bill, harn't left the roads, with oranges and nuts!

MRS. F.

If seas have roads, they 're very rough — I never felt such ruts!

BOATMAN.

It 's neap, ye see, she 's heavy lade, and could n't pass the bar.

MRS. F.

The bar! what, roads with turnpikes too? I wonder where they are!

BOATMAN.

Ho! Brig ahoy! hard up! hard up! that lubber cannot steer!

MRS. F.

Yes, yes,— hard up upon a rock! I know some danger 's near!
Lord, there 's a wave! it 's coming in! and roar-[ing like a bull!

BOATMAN.

Nothing, Ma'am, but a little slop! go large, Bill! keep her full!

MRS. F.

What, keep her full! what daring work! when full, she must go down!

BOATMAN.

Why, Bill, it lulls! ease off a bit — it 's coming off the town!
Steady your helm! we 'll clear the *Pint!* lay right for yonder pink!

MRS. F.

Be steady — well, I hope they can! but they 've got a pint of drink!

BOATMAN.

Bill, give that sheet another haul — she 'll fetch it up this reach.

MRS. F.

I 'm getting rather pale, I know, and they see it by that speech!

I wonder what it is, now, but —— I never felt so queer!

BOATMAN.

Bill, mind your luff — why Bill, I say, she's yawing — keep her near!

MRS. F.

Keep near! we're going further off; the land's behind our backs.

BOATMAN.

Be easy, Ma'am, it's all correct, that's only 'cause we tacks:
We shall have to beat about a bit,— Bill, keep her out to see.

MRS. F.

Beat who about? keep who at sea? — how black they look at me!

BOATMAN.

It's veering round — I knew it would! off with her head! stand by!

MRS. F.

Off with her head! whose? where? what with? — an axe I seem to spy!

BOATMAN.

She can't not keep her own, you see; we shall have to pull her in!

MRS. F.

They 'll drown me, and take all I have! my life 's not worth a pin!

BOATMAN.

Look out you know, be ready, Bill — just when she takes the sand!

MRS. F.

The sand — O Lord! to stop my mouth! how every thing is planned!

BOATMAN.

The handspike, Bill — quick, bear a hand! now Ma'am, just step ashore!

MRS. F.

What! ain't I going to be killed — and weltered in my gore?
Well, Heaven be praised! but I 'll not go a sailing any more!

LITERARY AND LITERAL.

THE March of Mind upon its mighty stilts,
(A spirit by no means to fasten mocks on,)
In travelling through Berks, Beds, Notts, and
Wilts,
Hants — Bucks, Herts, Oxon,
Got up a thing our ancestors ne'er thought on,
A thing that, only in our proper youth,
We should have chuckled at — in sober truth,
A Conversazione at Hog's Norton!

A place whose native dialect, somehow,
Has always by an adage been affronted,
And that it is all *gutterals*, is now
Taken for grunted.

Conceive the snoring of a greedy swine,
The slobbering of a hungry Ursine Sloth —
If you have ever heard such creature dine —
And — for Hog's Norton, make a mix of both! —

O shades of Shakspeare! Chaucer! Spenser!
Milton! Pope! Gray! Warton!
O Colman! Kenny! Planche! Poole! Peake!
Pocock! Reynolds! Morton!

O Grey! Peel! Sadler! Wilberforce! Burdett!
Hume! Wilmot Horton!
Think of your prose and verse, and worse — delivered in
Hog's Norton! —

The founder of Hog's Norton Athenæum
Framed her society
With some variety
From Mr. Roscoe's Liverpool museum;
Not a mere pic-nic, for the mind's repast,
But, tempting to the solid knife-and-forker,
It held its sessions in the house that last
Had killed a porker.

It chanced one Friday,
One Farmer Grayley stuck a very big hog,
A perfect Gog or Magog of a pig-hog,
Which made of course a literary high day, ——
Not that our Farmer was a man to go
With literary tastes — so far from suiting 'em,
When he heard mention of Professor *Crowe*,
Or Lalla-*Rookh*, he always was for shooting 'em!
In fact in letters he was quite a log,
With him great Bacon
Was literally taken,
And Hogg — the Poet — nothing but a Hog!
As to all others on the list of Fame,
Although they were discussed and mentioned daily,

He only recognized one classic name, [*Baillie!*
And thought that *she* had hung herself — *Miss*

To balance this, our Farmer's only daughter
Had a great taste for the Castalian water —
A Wordsworth worshipper — a Southey wooer,—
(Though men that deal in water-color cakes
May disbelieve the fact — yet nothing 's truer)
She got the *bluer*
The more she dipped and dabbled in the *Lakes*.
The secret truth is, Hope, the old deceiver,
At future Authorship was apt to hint,
Producing what some call the *Type-us* Fever,
Which means a burning to be seen in print.

Of learning's laurels — Miss Joanna Baillie —
Of Mrs. Hemans — Mrs. Wilson — daily
Dreamt Anne Priscilla Isabella Grayley;
And Fancy hinting that she had the better
Of L. E. L. by one initial letter,
She thought the world would quite enraptured see

"LOVE LAYS AND LYRICS

BY

A. P. I. G."

Accordingly, with very great propriety,
She joined the H. N. B. and double S.,

That is,— Hog's Norton Blue Stocking Society;
And saving when her Pa. his pigs prohibited,
Contributed
Her pork and poetry towards the mess.

This feast, we said, one Friday was the case,
When farmer Grayley — from Macbeth to quote —
Screwing his courage to the "sticking place,"
Stuck a large knife into a grunter's throat: —
A kind of murder that the law's rebuke
Seldom condemns by shake of its peruke,
Showing the little sympathy of *big-wigs*
With *pig-wigs!*

The swine — poor wretch! — with nobody to speak for it,
And beg its life, resolved to have a squeak for it;
So — like the fabled swan — died singing out,
And, thus, there issued from the farmer's yard
A note that notified without a card,
An invitation to the evening rout.

And when the time came duly,— "at the close of
The day," as Beattie has it, "when the ham — "
Bacon, and pork were ready to dispose of,
And pettitoes and chit'lings too, to cram,—
Walked in the H. N. B. and double S.'s
All in appropriate and swinish dresses,
For lo! it is a fact, and not a joke,

Although the Muse might fairly jest upon it,
They came—each "Pig-faced Lady," in that bonnet
We call *a poke.*
The Members all assembled thus, a rare woman
At pork and poetry was chosen *chairwoman;*—
In fact, the bluest of the Blues, Miss Ikey,
Whose whole pronunciation was so piggy,
She always named the authoress of "*Psyche,*"—
As Mrs. *Tiggey!*

And now arose a question of some moment,—
What author for a lecture was the richer,
Bacon or Hogg? there were no votes for Beaumont,
But some for *Flitcher;*
While others, with a more sagacious reasoning,
Proposed another work,
And thought their pork
Would prove more relishing from Thomson's Season-ing!

But, practised in Shaksperian readings daily,—
O! Miss Macaulay! Shakspeare at Hog's Norton!—
Miss Anne Priscilla Isabella Grayley
Selected *him* that evening to snort on.
In short, to make our story not a big tale,
Just fancy her exerting
Her talents, and converting

The Winter's Tale to something like a pig-tale!
Her sister auditory,
All sitting round, with grave and learned faces,
Were very plauditory,
Of course, and clapped her at the proper places;
Till fanned at once by fortune and the Muse,
She thought herself the blessedest of Blues.
But Happiness, alas! has blights of ill,
And Pleasure's bubbles in the air explode; —
There is no travelling through life but still
The heart will meet with breakers on the road!

With that peculiar voice
Heard only from Hog's Norton throats and noses,
Miss G., with Perdita, was making choice
Of buds and blossoms for her summer posies,
When coming to that line, where Proserpine
Lets fall her flowers from the wain of Dis;
Imagine this —
Uprose on his hind legs old Farmer Grayley,
Grunting this question for the club's digestion,
"Do *Dis's Wagon* go from the Ould Bäaley?"

ODE TO PERRY.

THE INVENTOR OF THE PATENT PERRYAN PEN.

"In this good work, Penn appears the greatest, usefullest of God's instruments. Firm and unbending when the exigency requires it — soft and yielding when rigid inflexibility is not a desideratum,— fluent and flowing, at need, for eloquent rapidity — slow and retentive in cases of deliberation — never spluttering or by amplification going wide of the mark — never splitting, if it can be helped, with any one, but ready to wear itself out rather in their service — all things as it were with all men,— ready to embrace the hand of Jew, Christian, or Mahometan,— heavy with the German, light with the Italian, oblique with the English, upright with the Roman, backward in coming forward with the Hebrew,— in short, for flexibility, amiability, constitutional durability, general ability, and universal utility, it would be hard to find a parallel to the great Penn."

PERRY'S CHARACTERISTICS OF A SETTLER.

I.

O! PATENT, Pen-inventing Perryan Perry!
Friend of the Goose and Gander,
That now unplucked of their quill-feathers wander,
Cackling, and gabbling, dabbling, making merry,

About the happy Fen,
Untroubled for one pennyworth of pen,
For which they chant thy praise all Britain
through,
From Goose-Green unto Gander-Cleugh!—

II.

Friend to all Author-kind—
Whether of Poet or of Proser,—
Thou art composer unto the composer
Of pens,—yea, patent vehicles for Mind
To carry it on jaunts, or more extensive
*Perry*grinations through the realms of Thought;
Each plying from the Comic to the Pensive,
An Omnibus of intellectual sort!

III.

Modern Improvements in their course we feel;
And while to iron-railroads heavy wares,
Dry goods, and human bodies, pay their fares,
Mind flies on steel,
To Penrith, Penrhyn, even to Penzance.
Nay, penetrates, perchance,
To Pennsylvania, or, without rash vaunts,
To where the Penguin haunts!

IV.

In times bygone, when each man cut his quill,
With little Perryan skill,

What horrid, awkward, bungling tools of trade
Appeared the writing implements home-made!
What Pens were sliced, hewed, hacked, and haggled out,
Slit or unslit, with many a various snout,
Aquiline, Roman, crooked, square, and snubby,
Stumpy and stubby;
Some capable of ladye-billets neat,
Some only fit for Ledger-keeping Clerk,
And some to grub down Peter Stubbs his mark,
Or smudge through some illegible receipt;
Others in florid caligraphic plans,
Equal to Ships, and wiggy Heads, and Swans!

V.

To try in any common inkstands, then,
With all their miscellaneous stocks,
To find a decent pen,
Was like a dip into a lucky box:
You drew,— and got one very curly,
And split like endive in some hurly-burly;
The next, unslit, and square at end, a spade;
The third, incipient pop-gun, not yet made;
The fourth a broom; the fifth of no avail,
Turned upwards, like a rabbit's tail;
And last, not least, by way of a relief,
A stump that Master Richard, James, or John,
Had tried his candle-cookery upon,
Making "roast-beef!"

VI

Not so thy Perryan Pens!
True to their M's and N's,
They do not with a whizzing zigzag split,
Straddle, turn up their noses, sulk, and spit,
Or drop large dots,
Huge fullstop blots,
Where even semicolons were unfit.
They will not frizzle up, or, broom-like, drudge
In sable sludge —
Nay, bought at proper "Patent Perryan" shops,
They write good grammar, sense, and mind their stops;
Compose both prose and verse, the sad or merry —
For when the Editor, whose pains compile
The grown-up Annual, or the Juvenile,
Vaunteth his articles, not women's, men's,
But lays "by the most celebrated Pens,"
What means he but thy Patent Pens, my Perry?

VII.

Pleasant they are to feel!
So firm! so flexible! composed of steel
So finely tempered — fit for tenderest Miss
To give her passion breath,
Or Kings to sign the warrant stern of death —
But their supremest merit still is this,

Write with them all your days,
Tragedy, Comedy, all kinds of plays —
(No Dramatist should ever be without 'em) —
And, just conceive the bliss,—
There is so little of the goose about 'em,
One 's safe from any hiss!

VIII.

Ah! who can paint that first great awful night,
Big with a blessing or a blight,
When the poor Dramatist, all fume and fret,
Fuss, fidget, fancy, fever, funking, fright,
Ferment, fault-fearing, faintness — more f's yet:
Flushed, frigid, flurried, flinching, fitful, flat,—
Add famished, fuddled, and fatigued, to that;
Funeral, fate-foreboding — sits in doubt,
Or rather doubt with hope, a wretched marriage,
To see his Play upon the stage come out;
No stage to him! it is Thalia's carriage,
And he is sitting on the spikes behind it,
Striving to look as if he didn't mind it!

IX.

Witness how Beazley vents upon his hat
His nervousness, meanwhile his fate is dealt:
He kneads, moulds, pummels it, and sits it flat,
Squeezes and twists it up, until the felt
That went a Beaver in, comes out a Rat!
Miss Mitford had mis-givings, and in fright,
Upon Rienzi's night,

Gnawed up one long kid glove, and all her bag,
Quite to a rag.
Knowles has confessed he trembled as for life,
Afraid of his own "Wife;
Poole told me that he felt a monstrous pail
Of water backing him, all down his spine,—
"The ice-brook's temper"—pleasant to the chine!—
For fear that Simpson and his Co. should fail.
Did Lord Glengall not frame a mental prayer,
Wishing devoutly he was Lord knows-where?
Nay, did not Jerrold, in enormous drouth,
While doubtful of Nell Gwynne's eventful luck,
Squeeze out and suck
More oranges with his one fevered mouth,
Than Nelly had to hawk from North to South?
Yea, Buckstone, changing color like a mullet,
Refused, on an occasion, once, twice, thrice,
From his best friend, an ice,
Lest it should hiss in his own red-hot gullet!

X.

Doth punning Peake not sit upon the points
Of his own jokes, and shake in all his joints,
During their trial?
'Tis past denial.
And does not Pocock, feeling, like a peacock,
All eyes upon him turn to very meacock?
And does not Planché, tremulous and blank,
Meanwhile his personages tread the boards,

Seem goaded by sharp swords,
And called upon himself to "walk the plank?"
As for the Dances, Charles and George to boot,
What have they more
Of ease and rest, for sole of either foot,
Than bear that capers on a hotted floor?

XI.

Thus pending — does not Mathews, at sad shift
For voice, croak like a frog in waters fenny? —
Serle seem upon the surly seas adrift? —
And Kenny think he 's going to Kilkenny? —
Haynes Bayley feel Old ditto, with the note
Of Cotton in his ear, a mortal grapple
About his arms, and Adam's apple,
Big as a fine Dutch codling, in his throat?
Did Rodwell, on his chimney-piece, desire
Or not to take a jump into the fire?
Did Wade feel as composed as music can?
And was not Bernard his own Nervous Man?
Lastly, don't Farley, a bewildered elf,
Quake at the Pantomime he loves to cater,
And ere its changes ring, transform himself? —
A frightful mug of human delf?
A spirit-bottle — empty of "the cratur"?
A leaden-platter ready for the shelf?
A thunderstruck dumb-waiter?

XII.

To clench the fact,
Myself, once guilty, of one small rash act,
Committed at the Surrey
Quite in a hurry,
Felt all this flurry,
Corporal worry,
And spiritual scurry,
Dram-devil — attic curry!
All going well,
From prompter's bell,
Until befell
A hissing at some dull imperfect dunce —
There 's no denying,
I felt in all four elements at once!
My head was swimming, while my arms were flying,
My legs for running — all the rest was frying!

XIII.

Thrice welcome, then, for this peculiar use
Thy pens so innocent of goose!
For this shall Dramatists, when they make merry,
Discarding Port and Sherry,
Drink — "Perry!"
Perry, whose fame, pennated, is let loose
To distant lands,
Perry, admitted on all hands,
Text, running, German, Roman,
For Patent Perryans approached by no man!

And when, ah, me! far distant be the hour!
Pluto shall call thee to his gloomy bower,
Many shall be thy pensive mourners, many!
And Penury itself shall club its penny,
To raise thy monument in lofty place;
Higher than York's, or any son of War;
Whilst Time all meaner effigies shall bury,
        On due pentagonal base,
Shall stand the Parian, Perryan, perriwiged
    Perry,
Perched on the proudest peak of Penman Mawr!

THE UNDYING ONE.

"He shall not die." — UNCLE TOBY.

I.

OF all the verses, grave or gay,
  That ever wiled an hour,
I never knew a mingled lay
  At once so sweet and sour,
As that by Ladye Norton spun,
And christened the "Undying One."

II.

I'm very certain that she drew
  A portrait, when she penned

That picture of a perfect Jew,
  Whose days will never end:
I 'm sure it means my Uncle Lunn,
For he is an Undying One.

III.

These twenty years he 's been the same,
  And may be twenty more;
But Memory's Pleasures only claim
  His features for a score;
Yet in that time the change is none —
The image of th' Undying One!

IV.

They say our climate 's damp and cold,
  And lungs are tender things;
My uncle 's much abroad and old,
  But when "King Cole" he sings,
A Stentor's voice, enough to stun,
Declares him an Undying One.

V.

Others have died from needle-pricks,
  And very slender blows;
From accidental slips or kicks,
  Or bleedings at the nose;
Or choked by grape-stone, or a bun —
But he is the Undying One!

VI.

A soldier once, he once endured
A bullet in the breast —
It might have killed — but only cured
An asthma in the chest;
He was not to be slain with gun,
For he is the Undying One.

VII.

In water once too long he dived,
And all supposed him beat,
He seemed so cold — but he revived
To have another heat,
Just when we thought his race was run,
And came in fresh — th' Undying One!

VIII.

To look at Meux's once he went,
And tumbled in the vat —
And greater Jobs their lives have spent
In lesser boils than that,—
He left the beer quite underdone,
No bier to the Undying One!

IX.

He 's been from strangulation black,
From bile, of yellow hue,
Scarlet from fever's hot attack,
From cholera morbus blue;

Yet with these dyes — to use a pun —
He still is the Undying One.

X.

He rolls in wealth, yet has no wife
  His Three per Cents. to share;
He never married in his life,
  Or flirted with the fair;
The sex he made a point to shun,
For beauty an Undying One.

XI.

To judge him by the present signs,
  The future by the past,
So quick he lives, so slow declines,
  The Last Man won't be last,
But buried underneath a ton
Of mould by the Undying One!

XII.

Next Friday week his birthday boast,
  His ninetieth year he spends,
And I shall have his health to toast
  Amongst expectant friends,
And wish — it really sounds like fun —
Long life to the Undying One!

COCKLE *v.* CACKLE.

THOSE who much read advertisements and bills,
  Must have seen puffs of Cockle's Pills,
    Called Anti-bilious —
Which some Physicians sneer at, supercilious,
But which we are assured, if timely taken,
    May save your liver and bacon;
Whether or not they really give one ease,
    I, who have never tried,
    Will not decide;
But no two things in union go like these —
Viz: — Quacks and Pills — save Ducks and
    Pease.
Now Mrs. W. was getting sallow,
Her lilies not of the white kind, but yellow,
And friends portended was preparing for
    A human Pâté Périgord;
She was, indeed, so very far from well,
Her Son, in filial fear, procured a box
Of those said pellets to resist Bile's shocks,
And — tho' upon the ear it strangely knocks —
To save her by a Cockle from a shell!

But Mrs. W., just like Macbeth,
Who very vehemently bids us "throw

Bark to the Bow-wows," hated physic so,
It seemed to share "the bitterness of death:"
Rhubarb — Magnesia — Jalap, and the kind —
Senna — Steel — Assa-fœtida, and Squills —
Powder or Draught — but least her throat inclined
To give a course to Boluses or Pills;
No — not to save her life, in lung or lobe,
For all her lights' or all her liver's sake,
Would her convulsive thorax undertake,
Only one little uncelestial globe!

'T is not to wonder at, in such a case,
If she put by the pill-box in a place
For linen rather than for drugs intended —
Yet for the credit of the pills let 's say
After they thus were stowed away,
Some of the linen mended;
But Mrs. W. by disease's dint,
Kept getting still more yellow in her tint,
When lo! her second son, like elder brother,
Marking the hue on the parental gills,
Brought a new charge of Anti-tumeric Pills,
To bleach the jaundiced visage of his Mother —
Who took them — in her cupboard — like the other.

"Deeper and deeper, still," of course,
The fatal color daily grew in force;
Till daughter W. newly come from Rome,

Acting the self-same filial, pillial, part,
To cure Mamma, another dose brought home
Of Cockles ; — not the Cockles of her heart !
These going where the others went before,
Of course she had a very pretty store ;
And then — some hue of health her cheek adorning,
The Medicine so good must be,
They brought her dose on dose, which she
Gave to the up-stairs cupboard, " night and morning."
Till wanting room at last, for other stocks,
Out of the window one fine day she pitched
The pillage of each box, and quite enriched
The feed of Mister Burrell's hens and cocks,—
A little Barber of a by-gone day,
Over the way
Whose stock in trade, to keep the least of shops,
Was one great head of Kemble,— that is, John,
Staring in plaster, with a *Brutus* on,
And twenty little Bantam fowls — with *crops.*

Little Dame W. thought when through the sash
She gave the physic wings,
To find the very things
So good for bile, so bad for chicken rash,
For thoughtless cock and unreflecting pullet !
But while they gathered up the nauseous nubbles,
Each pecked itself into a peck of troubles,
And brought the hand of Death upon its gullet.

They might as well have addled been, or ratted,
For long before the night — ah woe betide
The Pills! each suicidal Bantam died
Unfatted!

Think of poor Burrell's shock,
Of Nature's debt to see his hens all payers,
And laid in death as Everlasting Layers,
With Bantam's small Ex-Emperor, the Cock,
In ruffled plumage and funereal hackle,
Giving, undone by Cockle, a last Cackle!
To see as stiff as stone, his un'live stock,
It really was enough to move his block.
Down on the floor he dashed, with horror big,
Mr. Bell's third wife's mother's coachman's wig;
And with a tragic stare like his own Kemble,
Burst out with natural emphasis enough,
And voice that grief made tremble,
Into that very speech of sad Macduff —
"What! — all my pretty chickens and their dam,
At one fell swoop! —
Just when I 'd bought a coop
To see the poor lamented creatures cram!"

After a little of this mood,
And brooding over the departed brood,
With razor he began to ope each craw,
Already turning black, as black as coals;
When lo! the undigested cause he saw —
"Pisoned by goles!"

To Mrs. W.'s luck a contradiction,
Her window still stood open to conviction;
And by short course of circumstantial labor,
He fixed the guilt upon his adverse neighbor;—
Lord! how he railed at her: declaring now,
He 'd bring an action ere next Term of Hilary,
Then, in another moment, swore a vow,
He 'd make her do pill-penance in the pillory!
She, meanwhile distant from the dimmest dream
Of combating with guilt, yard-arm or arm-yard,
Lapped in a paradise of tea and cream;
When up ran Betty with a dismal scream—
"Here 's Mr. Burrell, ma'am, with all his farm-
yard!"
Straight in he came, unbowing and unbending,
With all the warmth that iron and a barber
Can harbour;
To dress the head and front of her offending,
The fuming phial of his wrath uncorking;
In short, he made her pay him altogether,
In hard cash, very *hard*, for every feather,
Charging of course, each Bantam as a Dorking;
Nothing could move him, nothing make him sup-
ple,
So the sad dame unpocketing her loss,
Had nothing left but to sit hands across,
And see her poultry "going down ten couple."

Now birds by poison slain,
As venomed dart from Indian's hollow cane,

Are edible; and Mrs. W.'s thrift,—
She had a thrifty vein,—
Destined one pair for supper to make shift,—
Supper as usual at the hour of ten:
But ten o'clock arrived and quickly passed,
Eleven — twelve — and one o'clock at last,
Without a sign of supper even then!
At length, the speed of cookery to quicken,
Betty was called, and with reluctant feet,
Came up at a white heat —
"Well, never I see chicken like them chicken!
My saucepans, they have been a pretty while in 'em!
Enough to stew them, if it comes to that,
To flesh and bones, and perfect rags; but drat
Those Anti-biling Pills! there is no bile in 'em!"

THE SWEEP'S COMPLAINT.

"I like to meet a sweep — such as come forth with the dawn, or somewhat earlier, with their little professional notes, sounding like the *peep, peep*, of a young sparrow."— Essays of Elia.

——— "A voice cried Sweep no more!
Macbeth hath murdered sweep."— Shakspeare.

One morning ere my usual time
I rose, about the seventh chime,
When little stunted boys that climb
Still linger in the street;

And as I walked, I saw indeed
A sample of the sooty breed,
Though he was rather run to seed,
  In height above five feet.
A mongrel tint he seemed to take;
Poetic simile to make,
Day through his Martin 'gan to break,
  White overcoming jet.
From side to side he crossed oblique,
Like Frenchman who has friends to seek,
And yet no English word can speak,
  He walked upon the fret:
And while he sought the dingy job,
His laboring breast appeared to throb,
And half a hiccup half a sob
  Betrayed internal woe.
To cry the cry he had by rote
He yearned, but law forbade the note,
Like Chanticleer, with roupy throat,
  He gaped — but not a crow!
I watched him, and the glimpse I snatched
Disclosed his sorry eyelids patched
With red, as if the soot had catched
  That hung about the lid;
And soon I saw the tear-drop stray,
He did not care to brush away;
Thought I the cause he will betray —
  And thus at last he did.

Well, here 's a pretty go! here 's a Gagging Act, if ever there was a gagging!

But I'm bound the members as silenced us, in doing it had plenty of magging.
They had better send us all off, they had, to the School for the Deaf and Dumb,
To unlarn us our mother tongues, and to make signs and be regularly mum.

But they can't undo natur — as sure as ever the morning begins to peep,
Directly I open my eyes, I can't help calling out Sweep
As natural as the sparrows among the chimbley-pots that say Cheep!
For my own part I find my suppressed voice very uneasy,
And comparable to nothing but having your tissue stopt when you are sneezy.
Well, it's all up with us! tho' I suppose we musn't cry all up.
Here's a precious merry Christmas, I'm blest if I can earn either bit or sup!
If crying Sweep, of mornings, is going beyond quietness's border,
Them as pretends to be fond of silence oughn't to cry hear, hear, and order, order.
I wonder Mr. Sutton, as we've sut-on too, don't sympathize with us
As a Speaker what don't speak, and that's exactly our own cus.
God help us if we don't not cry, how are we to pursue our callings?

I 'm sure we 're not half so bad as other businesses
with their bawlings.
For instance, the general postmen, that at six
o'clock go about ringing,
And wake up all the babbies that their mothers
have just got to sleep with singing.
Greens oughtn't to be cried no more than blacks —
to do the unpartial job,
If they bring in a Sooty Bill, they ought to have
brought in a Dusty Bob.
Is a dustman's voice more sweet than ourn, when
he comes a seeking arter the cinders,
Instead of a little boy like a blackbird in spring,
singing merrily under your windows?
There 's the omnibus cads as plies in Cheapside,
and keeps calling out Bank and City;
Let his Worship, the Mayor, decide if our call of
Sweep is not just as pretty.
I can't see why the Jews should be let go about
crying Old Close thro' their hooky noses,
And Christian laws should be ten times more hard
than the old stone laws of Moses.
Why isn't the mouths of the muffin-men com-
pelled to be equally shut?
Why, because Parliament members eat muffins,
but they never eat no sut.
Next year there won't be any May-day at all, we
shan't have no heart to dance,
And Jack in the Green will go in black like
mourning for our mischance;

If we live as long as May, that 's to say, through the hard winter and pinching weather,
For I don't see how we 're to earn enough to keep body and soul together.
I only wish Mr. Wilberforce or some of them that pities the niggers,
Would take a peep down in our cellars, and look at our miserable starving figures,
A-sitting idle on our empty sacks, and all ready to eat each other.
And a brood of little ones crying for bread to a heart-breaking Father and Mother.
They haven't a rag of clothes to mend, if their mothers had thread and needles,
But crawl naked about the cellars, poor things, like a swarm of common black beadles.
If they 'd only inquired before passing the Act and taken a few such peeps,
I don't think that any real gentleman would have set his face against sweeps.
Climbing 's an ancient respectable art, and if History 's of any vally,
Was recommended by Queen Elizabeth to the great Sir Walter Raleigh,
When he wrote on a pane of glass how I 'd climb, if the way I only knew,
And she writ beneath, if your heart 's afeared, don't venture up the flue.
As for me I was always loyal, and respected all powers that are higher,

But how can I now say God save the King, if I
an't to be a Cryer?
There 's London milk, that 's one of the cries, even
on Sunday the law allows,
But ought black sweeps, that are human beasts, to
be worser off than black cows?
Do *we* go calling about, when it 's church time,
like the noisy Billingsgate vermin,
And disturb the parson with "All alive O!" in the
middle of a funeral sermon?
But the fish won't keep, not the mackarel won't,
is the cry of the Parliament elves,
Every thing, except the sweeps I think, is to be
allowed to keep themselves!
Lord help us! what 's to become of us if we
mustn't cry no more?
We shan't do for black mutes to go a standing at
a death's door.
And we shan't do to emigrate, no not even to the
Hottentot nations,
For as time wears on, our black will wear off, and
then think of our situations!
And we should not do, in lieu of black-a-moor
footmen, to serve ladies of quality nimbly,
For when we were drest in our sky-blue and
silver, and large frills, all clean and neat,
and white silk stockings, if they pleased to
desire us to sweep the hearth, we couldn't
resist the chimbley.

THE SUB-MARINE.

It was a brave and jolly wight,
  His cheek was baked and brown,
For he had been in many climes
  With captains of renown,
And fought with those who fought so well
  At Nile and Camperdown.

His coat it was a soldier coat,
  Of red with yellow faced,
But (merman-like) he looked marine
  All downward from the waist;
His trowsers were so wide and blue,
  And quite in sailor taste!

He put the rummer to his lips,
  And drank a jolly draught;
He raised the rummer many times —
  And ever as he quaffed,
The more he drank, the more the Ship
  Seemed pitching fore and aft!

The ship seemed pitching fore and aft,
  As in a heavy squall;

It gave a lurch and down he went,
  Head-foremost in his fall!
Three times he did not rise, alas!
  He never rose at all!

But down he went, right down at once,
  Like any stone he dived,
He could not see, or hear, or feel—
  Of senses all deprived!
At last he gave a look around
  To see where he arrived!

And all that he could see was green,
  Sea-green on every hand!
And then he tried to sound beneath,
  And all he felt was sand!
There he was fain to lie, for he
  Could neither sit nor stand!

And lo! above his head there bent
  A strange and staring lass!
One hand was in her yellow hair,
  The other held a glass;
A mermaid she must surely be
  If ever mermaid was!

Her fish-like mouth was opened wide,
  Her eyes were blue and pale,
Her dress was of the ocean green,
  When ruffled by a gale;

Thought he "beneath that petticoat
  She hides a salmon-tail!"

She looked as siren ought to look,
  A sharp and bitter shrew,
To sing deceiving lullabies
  For mariners to rue,—
But when he saw her lips apart,
  It chilled him through and through!

With either hand he stopped his ears
  Against her evil cry;
Alas, alas, for all his care,
  His doom it seemed to die,
Her voice went ringing through his head
  It was so sharp and high!

He thrust his fingers further in
  At each unwilling ear,
But still, in very spite of all,
  The words were plain and clear:
"I can't stand here the whole day long,
  To hold your glass of beer!"

With opened mouth and opened eyes,
  Up rose the Sub-marine,
And gave a stare to find the sands
  And deeps where he had been:
There was no siren with her glass!
  No waters ocean-green!

The wet deception from his eyes
  Kept fading more and more,
He only saw the bar-maid stand
  With pouting lip before —
The small green parlor of The Ship,
  And little sanded floor!

DOG-REL VERSES, BY A POOR BLIND.

"Hark! hark! the dogs do bark,
  The beggars are coming . . ." — OLD BALLAD.

OH what shall I do for a dog?
  Of sight I have not got a particle,
    Globe, Standard, or Sun,
    Times, Chronicle — none
Can give *me* a good leading article.

A Mastiff once led me about,
  But people appeared so to fear him —
    I might have got pence
    Without his defence,
But Charity would not come near him.

A Bloodhound was not much amiss,
  But instinct at last got the upper;
    And tracking Bill Soames,
    And thieves to their homes,
I never could get home to supper.

A Fox-hound once served me as guide,
  A good one at hill and at valley;
    But day after day
    He led me astray,
To follow a milk-woman's tally.

A turnspit once did me good turns
  At going and crossing, and stopping;
    Till one day his breed
    Went off at full speed,
To spit at a great fire in Wapping.

A Pointer once pointed my way,
  But did not turn out quite so pleasant,
    Each hour I 'd a stop
    At a Poulterer's shop
To point at a very high pheasant.

A Pug did not suit me at all,
  The feature unluckily rose up;
    And folks took offence
    When offering pence,
Because of his turning his nose up.

A Butcher once gave me a dog,
  That turned out the worst one of any;
    A Bull-dog's own pup,
    I got a toss up,
Before he had brought me a penny.

My next was a Westminster Dog,
  From Aistrop the regular cadger;
    But, sightless, I saw
    He never would draw
A blind man so well as a badger.

A greyhound I got by a swop,
  But, Lord! we soon came to divorces:
    He treated my strip
    Of cord like a slip,
And left me to go my own courses.

A poodle once towed me along,
  But always we came to one harbor;
    To keep his curls smart,
    And shave his hind part,
He constantly called on a barber.

My next was a Newfoundland brute,
  As big as a calf fit for slaughter;
    But my old cataract
    So truly he backed
I always fell into the water.

I once had a sheep-dog for guide,
  His worth did not value a button;
    I found it no go,
    A Smithfield Ducrow,
To stand on four saddles of mutton.

My next was an Esquimaux dog,
A dog that my bones ache to talk on,
For picking his ways
On cold frosty days
He picked out the slides for a walk on.

Bijou was a lady-like dog,
But vexed me at night not a little,
When tea-time was come
She would not go home,
Her tail had once trailed a tin kettle.

I once had a sort of a Shock,
And kissed a street post like a brother,
And lost every tooth
In learning this truth —
One blind cannot well lead another.

A terrier was far from a trump,
He had one defect, and a thorough,
I never could stir,
'Od rabbit the cur!
Without going into the Borough.

My next was Dalmatian, the dog!
And led me in danger, oh crikey!
By chasing horse heels,
Between carriage wheels,
Till I came upon boards that were spiky.

The next that I had was from Cross,
  And once was a favourite spaniel
    With Nero, now dead,
    And so I was led
Right up to his den like a Daniel.

A mongrel I tried, and he did,
  As far as the profit and lossing,
    Except that the kind
    Endangers the blind,
The breed is so fond of a crossing.

A setter was quite to my taste,
  In alleys or streets broad or narrow,
    Till one day I met
    A very dead set,
At a very dead horse in a barrow.

I once had a dog that went mad,
  And sorry I was that I got him ;
    It came to a run,
    And a man with a gun
Peppered *me* when he ought to have shot him.

My profits have gone to the dogs,
  My trade has been such a deceiver,
    I fear that my aim
    Is a mere losing game,
Unless I can find a Retriever.

THE KANGAROOS.

A FABLE.

A PAIR of married kangaroos
  (The case is oft a human one too)
Were greatly puzzled once to choose
  A trade to put their eldest son to:
A little brisk and busy chap,
  As all the little K.'s just then are —
About some two months off the lap,—
  They 're not so long in arms as men are.

A twist in each parental muzzle
Betrayed the hardship of the puzzle —
  So much the flavor of life's cup
Is framed by early wrong or right,
And Kangaroos we know are quite
  Dependent on their "rearing up."
The question, with its ins and outs,
Was intricate and full of doubts ;
  And yet they had no squeamish carings
For trades unfit or fit for gentry,
Such notion never had an entry,
  For they had no armorial bearings.
Howbeit they 're not the last on earth
That might indulge in pride of birth ;

Whoe'er has seen their infant young
Bob in and out their mother's pokes,
Would own, with very ready tongue,
They are not born like common folks
Well, thus the serious subject stood,
It kept the old pair watchful nightly,
Debating for young hopeful's good,
That he might earn his livelihood,
And go through life (like them) uprightly.

Arms would not do at all; no, marry,
In that line all his race miscarry;
And agriculture was not proper,
Unless they meant the lad to tarry
Forever as a mere clod-hopper.
He was not well cut out for preaching,
At least in any striking style:
And as for being mercantile —
He was not formed for over-reaching.
The law — why there still fate ill-starred him,
And plainly from the bar debarred him:
A doctor — who would ever fee him?
In music he could scarce engage,
And as for going on the stage
In tragic socks I think I see him!
He would not make a rigging-mounter;
A haberdasher had some merit,
But there the counter still ran counter,
For just suppose
A lady chose
To ask him for a yard of ferret!

A gardener digging up his beds,
The puzzled parents shook their heads.
" A tailor would not do because —"
They paused and glanced upon his paws.
Some parish post,— though fate should place it
Before him, how could he embrace it ?
In short, each anxious Kangaroo
Discussed the matter through and through ;
By day they seemed to get no nearer,
          'Twas posing quite —
          And in the night
Of course they saw their way no clearer !
At last thus musing on their knees —
Or hinder elbows if you please —
It came — no thought was ever brighter !
In weighing every why and whether,
They jumped upon it both together —
" Let 's make the imp a *short-hand writer !* "

MORAL.

I wish all human parents so
  Would argue what their sons are fit for ;
Some would-be critics that I know
  Would be in trades they have more wit for

ODE FOR THE NINTH OF NOVEMBER.

O Lud! O Lud! O Lud!
I mean of course that venerable town,
Mentioned in stories of renown,
Built formerly of mud;—
O Lud, I say, why didst thou e'er
Invent the office of a Mayor,
An office that no useful purpose crowns,
But to set Aldermen against each other,
That should be Brother unto Brother,—
Sisters at least, by virtue of their gowns?

But still, if one must have a Mayor
To fill the Civic chair,
O Lud, I say,
Was there no better day
To fix on, than November Ninth so shivery
And dull for showing off the Livery's livery?
Dimming, alas!
The Brazier's brass,
Soiling the Embroiderers and all the Saddlers,
Sopping the Furriers,
Draggling the Curriers,
And making Merchant Tailors dirty paddlers;

Drenching the Skinners' Company to the skin,
Making the crusty Vintner chiller,
And turning the Distiller
To cold without instead of warm within ; —
Spoiling the bran-new beavers
Of Wax-chandlers and Weavers,
Plastering the Plasterers and spotting Mercers,
Hearty November cursers —
And showing Cordwainers and dapper Drapers
Sadly in want of brushes and of scrapers ;
Making the Grocer's company not fit
For company a bit ;
Dying the Dyers with a dingy flood,
Daubing incorporated Bakers,
And leading the Patten-makers,
Over their very pattens in the mud,—
O Lud ! O Lud ! O Lud !

" This is a sorry sight,"
To quote Macbeth — but oh, it grieves me quite,
To see your Wives and Daughters in their plumes —
White plumes not white —
Sitting at open windows catching rheums,
Not " Angels ever bright and fair,"
But angels ever brown and sallow,
With eyes — you cannot see above one pair,
For city clouds of black and yellow —

And artificial flowers, rose, leaf, and bud,
Such sable lilies
And grim daffodilies
Drooping, but not for drought, O Lud! O Lud!

I may as well, while I'm inclined,
Just go through all the faults I find:
Oh Lud! then, with a better air, say June,
Could'st thou not find a better tune
To sound with trumpets, and with drums,
Than "See the Conquering Hero comes,"
When he who comes ne'er dealt in blood?
Thy May'r is not a War Horse, Lud,
That ever charged on Turk or Tartar,
And yet upon a march you strike
That treats him like —
A little French if I may martyr —
Lewis Cart-Horse or Henry Carter!

O Lud! I say
Do change your day
To some time when your Show can really show;
When silk can seem like silk, and gold can glow.
Look at your Sweepers, how they shine in May!
Have it when there 's a sun to gild the coach,
And sparkle in tiara — bracelet — brooch —
Diamond — or paste — of sister, mother, daughter;
When grandeur really may be grand —
But if thy Pageant's thus obscured by land —
O Lud! it 's ten times worse upon the water!

Suppose, O Lud, to show its plan,
I call, like Blue Beard's wife, to sister Anne,
Who 's gone to Beaufort Wharf with niece
and aunt,
To see what she can see — and what she can't;
Chewing a saffron bun by way of cud,
To keep the fog out of a tender lung,
While perched in a verandah nicely hung
Over a margin of thy own black mud,
O Lud!

Now Sister Anne, I call to thee,
Look out and see:
Of course about the bridge you view them rally
And sally,
With many a wherry, sculler, punt, and cutter;
The Fishmongers' grand boat, but not for butter,
The Goldsmiths' glorious galley,—
Of course you see the Lord Mayor's coach aquatic,
With silken banners that the breezes fan,
In gold all glowing,
And men in scarlet rowing,
Like Doge of Venice to the Adriatic;
Of course you see all this, O Sister Anne?

"No, I see no such thing!
I only see the edge of Beaufort Wharf,
With two coal lighters fastened to a ring;
And, dim as ghosts,
Two little boys are jumping over posts;
And something, further off,

That 's rather like the shadow of a dog,
And all beyond is fog.
If there be any thing so fine and bright,
To see it I must see by second sight.
Call this a Show? It is not worth a pin!
I see no barges row,
No banners blow;
The Show is merely a gallanty-show,
Without a lamp or any candle in."

But sister Anne, my dear,
Although you cannot see, you still may hear?
Of course you hear, I 'm very sure of that,
The "Water parted from the Sea" in C,
Or "Where the Bee sucks," set in B;
Or Huntsman's chorus from the Freyschutz frightful,
Or Handel's Water Music in A flat.
O music from the water comes delightful!
It sounds as nowhere else it can:
You hear it first
In some rich burst,
Then faintly sighing,
Tenderly dying,
Away upon the breezes, Sister Anne.

"There is no breeze to die on;
And all their drums and trumpets, flutes and harps,
Could never cut their way with ev'n three sharps
Through such a fog as this, you may rely on.

I think, but am not sure, I hear a hum,
Like a very muffled double drum,
And then a something faintly shrill,
Like Bartlemy Fair's old buzz at Pentonville.
And now and then hear a pop,
As if from Pedley's Soda Water shop.
I 'm almost ill with the strong scent of mud,
And, not to mention sneezing,
My cough is, more than usual, teasing;
I really fear that I have chilled my blood,
O Lud! O Lud! O Lud! O Lud! O Lud!"

RONDEAU.

[EXTRACTED FROM A WELL-KNOWN ANNUAL.]

O CURIOUS reader, didst thou ne'er
Behold a worshipful Lord May'r
Seated in his great civic chair
So dear?

Then cast thy longing eyes this way,
It is the ninth November day,
And in his new-born state survey
One here!

To rise from little into great
Is pleasant; but to sink in state
From high to lowly is a fate
Severe.

Too soon his shine is overcast,
Chilled by the next November blast;
His blushing honors only last
One year!

He casts his fur and sheds his chains,
And moults till not a plume remains —
The next impending May'r distrains
His gear.

He slips like water through a sieve —
Ah, could his little splendor live
Another twelvemonth — he would give
One ear!

SYMPTOMS OF OSSIFICATION.

"An indifference to tears, and blood, and human suffering, that could only belong to a *Boney-parte*."—LIFE OF NAPOLEON.

TIME was, I always had a drop
For any tale or sigh of sorrow;
My handkerchief I used to sop
Till often I was forced to borrow;

I don't know how it is, but now
My eyelids seldom want a drying;
The doctors, p'rhaps, could tell me how —
I fear my heart is ossifying!

O'er Goethe how I used to weep,
With turnip cheeks and nose of scarlet,
When Werter put himself to sleep
With pistols kissed and cleaned by Charlotte;
Self-murder is an awful sin,
No joke there is in bullets flying,
But now at such a tale I grin —
I fear my heart is ossifying!

The Drama once could shake and thrill
My nerves, and set my tears a stealing,
The Siddons then could turn at will
Each plug upon the main of feeling;
At Belvidera now I smile,
And laugh while Mrs. Haller 's crying;
'Tis odd, so great a change of style —
I fear my heart is ossifying!

That heart was such — some years ago,
To see a beggar quite would shock it,
And in his hat I used to throw
The quarter's savings of my pocket:
I never wish — as I did *then!* —
The means from my own purse supplying,
To turn them all to gentlemen: —
I fear my heart is ossifying!

We 've had some serious things of late,
Our sympathies to beg or borrow,
New melo-drames, of tragic fate,
And acts, and songs, and tales of sorrow;
Miss Zouch's case, our eyes to melt,
And sundry actors sad good-bye-ing,
But Lord! so little have I felt,
I 'm sure my heart is ossifying!

THE POACHER.

A SERIOUS BALLAD.

But a bold pheasantry, their country's pride,
That once destroyed can never be supplied.
GOLDSMITH.

BILL BLOSSOM was a nice young man,
And drove the Bury coach;
But bad companions were his bane,
And egged him on to poach.

They taught him how to net the birds,
And how to noose the hare;
And with a wiry terrier,
He often set a snare.

Each "shiny night" the moon was bright,
To park, preserve, and wood
He went, and kept the game alive,
By killing all he could.

Land-owners, who had rabbits, swore
That he had this demerit—
Give him an inch of warren, he
Would take a yard of ferret.

At partridges he was not nice;
And many, large and small,
Without Hall's powder, without lead,
Were sent to Leaden-Hall.

He did not fear to take a deer
From forest, park, or lawn;
And without courting lord or duke,
Used frequently to *fawn*.

Folks who had hares discovered snares—
His course they could not stop:
No barber he, and yet he made
Their hares a perfect crop.

To pheasant he was such a foe,
He tried the keeper's nerves;
They swore he never seemed to have
Jam satis of *preserves*.

The Shooter went to beat, and found
  No sporting worth a pin,
Unless he tried the *covers* made
  Of silver, plate, or tin.

In Kent the game was little worth,
  In Surrey not a button;
The Speaker said he often tried
  The *Manors* about *Sutton.**

No county from his tricks was safe;
  In each he tried his lucks,
And when the keepers were in *Beds*,
  He often was at *Bucks*.

And when he went to *Bucks*, alas!
  They always came to *Herts*;
And even *Oxon* used to wish
  That he had his deserts.

But going to his usual *Hants*,
  Old *Cheshire* laid his plots:
He got entrapped by legal *Berks*,
  And lost his life in *Notts*.

* [Charles Manners Sutton was for many years Speaker of the House of Commons.]

I CANNOT BEAR A GUN.

"Timidity is generally reckoned an essential attribute of the fair sex, and this absurd notion gives rise to more false starts, than a race for the Leger. Hence screams at mice, fits at spiders, faces at toads, jumps at lizards, flights from daddy longlegs, panics at wasps, *sauve qui peut* at sight of a gun. Surely, when the military exercise is made a branch of education at so many ladies' academies, the use of the musket would only be a judicious step further in the march of mind. I should not despair, in a month's practice, of making the most timid British female fond of small arms." — HINTS BY A CORPORAL.

IT can't be minced, I 'm quite convinced,
All girls are full of flam,
Their feelings fine and feminine
Are nothing else but sham.
On all their tricks I need not fix,
I 'll only mention one,
How many a Miss will tell you this,
"I cannot bear a gun!"

There 's cousin Bell can't 'bide the smell
Of powder — horrid stuff!
A single pop will make her drop,
She shudders at a puff.

My Manton near, with aspen fear
  Will make her scream and run:
"It's always so, you brute, you know
  I cannot bear a gun!"

About my flask I must not ask,
  I must not wear a belt,
I must not take a punch to make
  My pellets, card or felt;
And if I just allude to dust,
  Or speak of number one,
"I beg you'll not — don't talk of shot,
  I cannot bear a gun!"

Percussion cap I dare not snap,
  I may not mention Hall,
Or raise my voice for Mr. Joyce,
  His wadding to recall;
At Hawker's book I must not look,
  All shooting I must shun,
Or else — "It's hard, you've no regard,
  I cannot bear a gun!"

The very dress I wear, no less
  Must suit her timid mind,
A blue or black must clothe my back,
  With swallow-tails behind;
By fustian, jean, or velveteen,
  Her nerves are overdone:
"O do not, John, put gaiters on,
  I cannot bear a gun!"

Ev'n little James she snubs, and blames
His Lilliputian train,
Two inches each from mouth to breech,
And charged with half a grain —
His crackers stopped, his squibbing dropped,
He has no fiery fun,
And all thro' her "How dare you, Sir?
I cannot bear a gun!"

Yet Major Flint,— the Devil 's in 't!
May talk from morn to night,
Of springing mines, and twelves and nines,
And volleys left and right,
Of voltigeurs and tirailleurs,
And bullets by the ton:
She never dies of fright, or cries
"I cannot bear a gun!"

It stirs my bile to see her smile
At all his bang and whiz,
But if I talk of morning walk,
And shots as good as his,
I must not name the fallen game:
As soon as I 've begun,
She 's in her pout, and crying out,
"I cannot bear a gun!"

Yet, underneath the rose, her teeth
Are false, to match her tongue:
Grouse, partridge, hares, she never spares,
Or pheasants, old or young —

On widgeon, teal, she makes a meal,
  And yet objects to none:
"What have I got, it 's full of shot!
  I cannot bear a gun!"

At pigeon-pie she is not shy,
  Her taste it never shocks,
Though they should be from Battersea,
  So famous for blue rocks;
Yet when I bring the very thing
  My marksmanship has won,
She cries "Lock up that horrid cup,
  I cannot bear a gun!"

Like fool and dunce I got her once
  A box at Drury Lane,
And by her side I felt a pride
  I ne'er shall feel again:
To read the bill it made her ill,
  And this excuse she spun,
"Der Freyschütz, O, seven shots! you know,
  I cannot bear a gun!"

Yet at a hint from Major Flint,
  Her very hands she rubs,
And quickly drest in all her best,
  Is off to Wormwood Scrubbs.
The whole review she sits it through,
  With noise enough to stun,
And never winks, or even thinks,
  "I cannot bear a gun!"

She thus may blind the Major's mind
In mock-heroic strife,
But let a bout at war break out,
And where 's the soldier's wife,
To take his kit and march a bit
Beneath a broiling sun?
Or will she cry, "My dear, good-by,
I cannot bear a gun!"

If thus she dotes on army coats,
And regimental cuffs,
The yeomanry might surely be
Secure from her rebuffs;
But when I don my trappings on,
To follow Captain Dunn,
My carbine's gleam provokes a scream
"I cannot bear a gun!"

It can't be minced, I 'm quite convinced,
All girls are full of flam,
Their feelings fine and feminine
Are nothing else but sham;
On all their tricks I need not fix,
I 'll only mention one,
How many a Miss will tell you this,
"I cannot bear a gun!"

TRIMMER'S EXERCISE,

FOR THE USE OF CHILDREN.

Here, come, Master Timothy Todd,
  Before we have done you 'll look grimmer;
You 've been spelling some time for the rod,
  And your jacket shall know I 'm a Trimmer.

You don't know your A from your B,
  So backward you are in your Primer:
Don't kneel — you shall go on *my* knee,
  For I 'll have you to know I 'm a Trimmer.

This morning you hindered the cook,
  By melting your dumps in the skimmer;
Instead of attending your book,—
  But I 'll have you to know I 'm a Trimmer.

To-day, too, you went to the pond,
  And bathed, though you are not a swimmer;
And with parents so doting and fond —
  But I 'll have you to know I 'm a Trimmer.

After dinner you went to the wine,
  And helped yourself — yes, to a brimmer ;
You couldn't walk straight in a line,
  But I 'll make you to know I 'm a Trimmer.

You kick little Tomkins about,
  Because he is slighter and slimmer ;
Are the weak to be thumped by the stout ?
  But I 'll have you to know I 'm a Trimmer.

Then you have a sly pilfering trick,
  Your school-fellows call you the nimmer,—
I will cut to the bone if you kick !
  For I 'll have you to know I 'm a Trimmer.

To-day you made game at my back :
  You think that my eyes are grown dimmer,
But I watched you, I 've got a sly knack !
  And I 'll have you to know I 'm a Trimmer.

Don't think that my temper is hot,
  It 's never beyond a slow simmer ;
I 'll teach you to call me Dame Trot,
  But I 'll have you to know I 'm a Trimmer.

Miss Edgeworth, or Mrs. Chapone,
  Might melt to behold your tears glimmer ;
Mrs. Barbauld would let you alone,
  But I 'll have you to know I 'm a Trimmer.

THE FOX AND THE HEN.

A FABLE.

Speaking within *compass*, as to fabulousness I prefer *Southcote* to *Northcote*. PIGROGROMITUS.

ONE day, or night, no matter where or when,
Sly Reynard, like a footpad, laid his pad
Right on the body of a speckled Hen,
Determined upon taking all she had;
And like a very bibber at his bottle,
Began to draw the claret from her throttle;
Of course it put her in a pretty pucker,
And with a scream as high
As she could cry,
She called for help — she had enough of sucker.

Dame Partlet's scream
Waked, luckily, the house-dog from his dream,
And, with a savage growl
In answer to the fowl,
He bounded forth against the prowling sinner,
And, uninvited, came to the Fox Dinner.
Sly Reynard, heedful of the coming doom,
Thought, self-deceived,
He should not be perceived,
Hiding his *brush* within a neighbouring *broom*;

But quite unconscious of a Poacher's snare,
And caught in copper noose,
And looking like a goose,
Found that his fate had "hung upon a *hare;*"
His tricks and turns were rendered of no use to him.
And, worst of all, he saw old surly Tray
Coming to play
Tray-Deuce with him.

Tray, an old Mastiff bred at Dunstable,
Under his Master, a most special constable,
Instead of killing Reynard in a fury,
Seized him for legal trial by a Jury;
But Juries — Æsop was a sheriff then —
Consisted of twelve Brutes and not of Men.

But first the Elephant sat on the body —
I mean the Hen — and próved that she was dead,
To the veriest fool's head
Of the Booby and the Noddy.
Accordingly, the Stork brought in a bill
Quite true enough to kill;
And then the Owl was called — for mark,
The Owl can witness in the dark.
To make the evidence more plain,
The Lynx connected all the chain.

In short there was no quirk or quibble
At which a legal Rat could nibble;

The Culprit was as far beyond hope's bounds,
As if the Jury had been *packed* — of hounds.
Reynard, however, at the utmost nick,
Is seldom quite devoid of shift and trick;
    Accordingly our cunning Fox,
Through certain influence, obscurely channelled,
A friendly Camel got into the box,
When 'gainst his life the Jury was impanelled.

Now, in the Silly Isles such is the law,
    If Jurors should withdraw,
They are to have no eating and no drinking,
Till all are starved into one way of thinking.

Thus Reynard's Jurors, who could not agree,
Were locked up strictly, without bit or mummock,
Till every Beast that only had *one* stomach,
Bent to the Camel, who was blest with *three.*
To do them justice, they debated
From four till ten, while dinner waited,
When thirst and hunger got the upper,
And each inclined to mercy, and hot supper:
"Not guilty" was the word, and Master Fox
Was freed to murder other hens and cocks.

MORAL.

What moral greets us by this tale's assistance
  But that the Solon is a sorry Solon,
Who makes the full stop of a Man's existence
  Depend upon a *Colon*?

THE COMET.

AN ASTRONOMICAL ANECDOTE.

"I cannot fill up a blank better than with a short history of this selfsame *Star*ling."

STERNE'S SENTIMENTAL JOURNEY.

AMONGST professors of astronomy,
Adepts in the celestial economy,
  The name of Herschel's very often cited:
And justly so, for he is hand and glove
With ev'ry bright intelligence above;
Indeed, it was his custom so to stop,
Watching the stars upon the house's top,
  That once upon a time he got be-knighted

In his observatory thus coquetting
  With Venus — or with Juno gone astray,
All sublunary matters quite forgetting
In his flirtations with the winking stars,
Acting the spy — it might be upon Mars —
      A new André;
Or, like a Tom of Coventry, sly peeping,
      At Dian sleeping;

Or ogling thro' his glass
Some heavenly lass
Tripping with pails along the Milky Way;
Or looking at that Wain of Charles the Martyr's: —
Thus he was sitting, watchman of the sky,
When lo! a something with a tail of flame
Made him exclaim,
"*My* stars!" — he always puts that stress on *my* —
"*My* stars and garters!"

"A comet, sure as I'm alive!
A noble one as I should wish to view;
It can't be Halley's though, *that* is not due
Till eighteen thirty-five.
Magnificent! — how fine his fiery trail!
Zounds! 'tis a pity, though he comes unsought —
Unasked — unreckoned, — in no human thought —
He ought — he ought — he ought
To have been caught
With scientific salt upon his tail!"

"I looked no more for it, I do declare,
Than the Great Bear!
As sure as Tycho Brahe is dead,
It really entered in my head,
No more than Berenice's Hair!"
Thus musing, Heaven's Grand Inquisitor
Sat gazing on the uninvited visiter

Till John, the serving-man, came to the upper
Regions, with "Please your Honour, come to
supper."

"Supper! good John, to-night I shall not sup
Except on that phenomenon — look up!"
"Not sup!" cried John, thinking with consternation
That supping on a *star* must be *star*vation,
Or ev'n to batten
On Ignes Fatui would never fatten.
His visage seemed to say,— that very odd is,—
But still his master the same tune ran on,
"I can't come down,— go to the parlour, John,
And say I'm supping with the heavenly bodies."

"The heavenly bodies!" echoed John, "Ahem!"
His mind still full of famishing alarms,
"'Zooks, if your Honour sups with *them*,
In helping, somebody must make long arms!"
He thought his master's stomach was in danger,
But still in the same tone replied the Knight,
"Go down, John, go, I have no appetite,
Say I'm engaged with a celestial stranger."—
Quoth John, not much *au fait* in such affairs,
"Wouldn't the stranger take a bit down stairs?

"No," said the master, smiling, and no wonder,
At such a blunder,
"The stranger is not quite the thing you think,
He wants no meat or drink,

And one may doubt quite reasonably whether
He has a mouth,
Seeing his head and tail are joined together,
Behold him,— there he is, John, in the South."

John looked up with his portentous eyes,
Each rolling like a marble in its socket.
At last the fiery tadpole spies,
And, full of Vauxhall reminiscence, cries,
"A rare good rocket!"

"A what! A rocket, John! Far from it!
What you behold, John, is a comet;
One of those most eccentric things
That in all ages
Have puzzled sages
And frightened kings;
With fear of change that flaming meteor, John,
Perplexes sovereigns, throughout its range"—
"Do he?" cried John;
"Well, let him flare on,
I haven't got no sovereigns to change!"

POMPEY'S GHOST.

A PATHETIC BALLAD.

"Skins may differ, but affection
Dwells in white and black the same."
COWPER.

'T WAS twelve o'clock, not twelve at night,
But twelve o'clock at noon;
Because the sun was shining bright
And not the silver moon.
A proper time for friends to call,
Or Pots, or Penny Post;
When, lo! as Phœbe sat at work,
She saw her Pompey's Ghost!

Now, when a female has a call
From people that are dead;
Like Paris ladies, she receives
Her visitors in bed.
But Pompey's spirit would not come
Like spirits that are white,
Because he was a Blackamoor,
And would n't show at night!

But of all unexpected things
  That happen to us here,
The most unpleasant is a rise
  In what is very dear.
So Phœbe screamed an awful scream
  To prove the seaman's text;
That after black appearances,
  White squalls will follow next.

"Oh, Phœbe, dear! oh, Phœbe, dear!
  Don't go to scream or faint;
You think because I'm black I am
  The Devil, but I ain't!
Behind the heels of Lady Lambe
  I walked while I had breath;
But that is past, and I am now
  A-walking after Death!

"No murder, though, I come to tell,
  By base and bloody crime;
So Phœbe, dear, put off your fits
  To some more fitting time.
No Coroner, like a boatswain's mate,
  My body need attack,
With his round dozen to find out
  Why I have died so black.

"One Sunday, shortly after tea,
  My skin began to burn
As if I had in my inside

A heater, like the urn.
Delirious in the night I grew,
And as I lay in bed,
They say I gathered all the wool
You see upon my head.

"His Lordship for his doctor sent,
My treatment to begin;—
I wish that he had called him out,
Before he called him in!
For though to physic he was bred,
And passed at Surgeon's Hall,
To make his post a sinecure
He never cured at all!

"The doctor looked about my breast,
And then about my back,
And then he shook his head and said
'Your case looks very black.'
And first he sent me hot cayenne
And then gamboge to swallow,
But still my fever would not turn
To Scarlet or to Yellow!

"With madder and with turmeric,
He made his next attack;
But neither he nor all his drugs
Could stop my dying black.
At last I got so sick of life,
And sick of being dosed,

One Monday morning I gave up
  My physic and the ghost!

"Oh, Phœbe, dear, what pain it was
  To sever every tie!
You know black beetles feel as much
  As giants when they die.
And if there is a bridal bed,
  Or bride of little worth,
It 's lying in a bed of mould,
  Along with Mother Earth.

"Alas; some happy, happy day,
  In church I hoped to stand,
And like a muff of sable skin
  Receive your lily hand.
But sternly with that piebald match,
  My fate untimely clashes,
For now, like Pompe-double-i,
  I 'm sleeping in my ashes!

"And now farewell! a last farewell!
  I 'm wanted down below,
And have but time enough to add
  One word before I go—
In mourning crape and bombazine
  Ne'er spend your precious pelf—
Don't go in black for me—for I
  Can do it for myself.

"Henceforth within my grave I rest,
But Death who there inherits,
Allowed my spirit leave to come,
You seemed so out of spirits:
But do not sigh, and do not cry,
By grief too much engrossed,
Nor for a ghost of color, turn
The color of a ghost!

"Again, farewell, my Phœbe, dear!
Once more a last adieu!
For I must make myself as scarce
As swans of sable hue."
From black to gray, from gray to nought,
The shape began to fade—
And, like an egg, though not so white,
The Ghost was newly laid!

EPIGRAM.

ON A LATE CATTLE SHOW IN SMITHFIELD.

Old Farmer Bull is taken sick,
Yet not with any sudden trick
Of fever, or his old dyspepsy;
But having seen the foreign stock,
It gave his system such a shock
He had a fit of cattle-epsy!

ODE TO THE PRINTER'S DEVIL,

WHO BROUGHT ME A PROOF TO BE CORRECTED, AND WHO FELL ASLEEP WHILE IT WAS UNDERGOING CORRECTION: BEING AN ODE FOUNDED ON FACT!

"Fallen Cherub!"—MILTON'S PARADISE LOST.

OH bright and blessed hour ;—
The Devil 's asleep !—I see his little lashes
Lying in sable o'er his sable cheek ;
Closed are his wicked little window-sashes,
And tranced is Evil's power !
The world seems hushed and dreaming out-a-doors,
  Spirits but speak ;
And the heart echoes, while the Devil snores.

Sleep, Baby of the damned !
Sleep, when no press of trouble standeth by !
Black wanderer amid the wandering,
  How quiet is thine eye !
Strange are thy very small pernicious dreams—
With shades of printers crammed,
And pica, double pica, on the wing !

Or in cold sheets thy sprite perchance is flying
  The world about—
Dying—and yet, not like the Devil dying—
  Dele,—the *Evil* out!.

Before sweet sleep drew down
The blinds upon thy *Day & Martin* eyes,
Thou did'st let slip thy slip of mischief on me,
With weary, weary sighs;
And then, outworn with *demoning* o'er town,
  Oblivion won thee!
Best of compositors! thou didst compose
Thy decent little wicked self, and go
A Devil-cruiser round the shores of sleep—
I hear thee fathom many a slumber-deep,
  In the waves of woe;
  Dropping thy lids of lead
  To sound the dead!

Heaven forgive me! I
Have wicked schemes about thee, wicked one;
And in my scheming, sigh
And stagger under a gigantic thought;
" What if I run my pen into thine eye,
And put thee out?
Killing the Devil will be a noble deed,
A deed to snatch perdition from mankind—
To make the Methodist's a stingless creed—
To root out terror from the Brewer's mind—
And break the bondage which the Printer presses—

To change the fate of Lawyers—
Confirm the Parson's holy sinecure—
Make worthless sin's approaches—
To justify the bringing up addresses
To me, in hackney coaches,
From operative Sawyers!"

"To murder thee"—
Methinks—"will never harm my precious head—
For what can chance me, when the Devil is dead?"
But when I look on thy serene repose,
Hear the small Satan dying through thy nose,
My thoughts become less dangerous and more
deep;
I can but wish thee everlasting sleep!
Sleep free from dreams
Of type, and ink, and press, and dabbing-ball—
Sleep free from all
That would make shadowy, devilish slumber
darker,
Sleep free from Mr. Baldwin's Mr. Parker!

Oh! fare thee well!
Farewell, black bit of breathing sin! Farewell,
Tiny remembrancer of a Printer's Hell!
Young thing of darkness, seeming
A small, poor *type* of wickedness *set up!*
Full is thy little cup
Of misery in the waking world! So dreaming
Perchance may now *undemonize* thy fate

And bear thee, Black-boy, to a whiter state!
Yet mortal evil is, than thine, more high;—
Thou art *upright* in sleep; men sleep—and *lie!*
And from thy lids to me a moral peeps,
For I correct my errors—while the Devil sleeps!

ANACREONTIC,

FOR THE NEW YEAR.

COME, fill up the Bowl, for if ever the glass
  Found a proper excuse, or fit season,
For toasts to be honored, or pledges to pass,
  Sure, this hour brings an exquisite reason:
For, hark! the last chime of the dial has ceased,
  And Old Time, who has leisure to cozen,
Having finished the months, like the flasks at a feast,
  Is preparing to tap a fresh dozen!
                    Hip! Hip! and Hurrah!

Then fill, all ye Happy and Free, unto whom
  The past Year has been pleasant and sunny;
Its months each as sweet as if made of the bloom
  Of the thyme whence the bee gathers honey—
Days ushered by dew-drops, instead of the tears,
  Maybe, wrung from some wretcheder cousin—

Then fill, and with gratitude join in the cheers
That triumphantly hail a fresh dozen!
Hip! Hip! and Hurrah!

And ye, who have met with Adversity's blast,
And been bowed to the earth by its fury;
To whom the Twelve Months, that have recently passed,
Were as harsh as a prejudiced jury—
Still, fill to the future! and join in our chime,
The regrets of remembrance to cozen,
And having obtained a New Trial of Time,
Shout, in hopes of a kindlier dozen!
Hip! Hip! and Hurrah!

EPIGRAM.

ON THE DEPRECIATED MONEY.

They may talk of the plugging and sweating
Of our coinage that's minted of gold,
But to me it produces no fretting
Of its shortness of weight to be told:
All the sov'reigns I'm able to levy
As to lightness can never be wrong,
But must surely be some of them heavy
For I never can carry them long.

TO C. DICKENS, ESQ.,

ON HIS DEPARTURE FOR AMERICA.

PSHAW! away with leaf and berry,
And the sober-sided cup!
Bring a goblet, and bright sherry,
And a bumper fill me up!
Though a pledge I had to shiver,
And the longest ever was!
Ere his vessel leaves our river,
I would drink a health to Boz!

Here 's success to all his antics,
Since it pleases him to roam,
And to paddle o'er Atlantics,
After such a *sale* at home!
May he shun all rocks whatever,
And each shallow sand that lurks,
And his *passage* be as clever
As the best among his works.

NOVEMBER.

No sun—no moon!
No morn—no noon—
No dawn—no dusk—no proper time of day—
No sky—no earthly view—
No distance looking blue—
No road—no street—no "t'other side the way"—
No end to any Row—
No indications where the Crescents go—
No top to any Steeple—
No recognitions of familiar people—
No Courtesies for showing 'em—
No knowing 'em!
No travelling at all—no locomotion,
No inkling of the way—no notion—
"No go"—by land or ocean—
No mail—no post—
No news from any foreign coast—
No park—no ring—no afternoon gentility—
No company—no nobility—
No warmth, no cheerfulness, no healthful ease,
No comfortable feel in any member—
No shade, no shine, no butterflies, no bees,
No fruits, no flowers, no leaves, no birds—
November!

END OF VOL. III.

CPSIA information can be obtained
at www.ICGtesting.com
Printed in the USA
LVHW110812120522
718525LV00003B/78

9 783375 002633